Little Jane
and the
Nameless Isle

A LITTLE JANE SILVER ADVENTURE

Little Jane

and the Nameless Isle

Adira Rotstein

DUNDURN
TORONTO

Editor: Allison Hirst
Design: Courtney Horner
Printer: Webcom

Library and Archives Canada Cataloguing in Publication

Rotstein, Adira, 1979-
  Little Jane and the nameless isle / Adira Rotstein.

"A little Jane Silver adventure".
Issued also in electronic formats.
ISBN 978-1-4597-0420-6

  I. Title.

PS8635.O78L57 2012   jC813'.6   C2012-900139-2

1   2   3   4   5   16   15   14   13   12

Conseil des Arts du Canada   Canada Council for the Arts   Canada   ONTARIO ARTS COUNCIL CONSEIL DES ARTS DE L'ONTARIO

We acknowledge the support of the **Canada Council for the Arts** and the **Ontario Arts Council** for our publishing program. We also acknowledge the financial support of the **Government of Canada** through the **Canada Book Fund** and **Livres Canada Books**, and the **Government of Ontario** through the **Ontario Book Publishing Tax Credit** and the **Ontario Media Development Corporation**.

Care has been taken to trace the ownership of copyright material used in this book. The author and the publisher welcome any information enabling them to rectify any references or credits in subsequent editions.

J. Kirk Howard, President

Printed and bound in Canada.
www.dundurn.com

Visit us at
Dundurn.com | Definingcanada.ca | @dundurnpress | Facebook.com/dundurnpress

Dundurn
3 Church Street, Suite 500
Toronto, Ontario, Canada
M5E 1M2

Gazelle Book Services Limited
White Cross Mills
High Town, Lancaster, England
LA1 4XS

Dundurn
2250 Military Road
Tonawanda, NY
U.S.A. 14150

To Mom and Dad who kept the faith,
who read to me and kept me safe

To my sweet, my Stevian Lee,
and all who loved and believed in me

To R.L.S. with a bottle of rum,
and to you dear readers, every one!

Chapter One

A Startling Scheme

Only a few days had passed since her parents' ship, the *Pieces of Eight*, was attacked and destroyed by pirate hunters, but to Little Jane Silver it already felt like years. Too much had happened in too short a time.

In the past few days everything had gone horribly wrong for Little Jane and her family. First, the bosun of the *Pieces of Eight*, Ned Ronk, had engineered a series of accidents that crippled the ship, pinning the blame on Little Jane. By the time her parents discovered Ned Ronk was working for pirate hunters, it was too late. A ship called the *Panacea* had overtaken them, set the *Pieces of Eight* on fire, and made off with her crew. Only Little Jane and Ishiro, the ship's cook, had escaped.

Now Little Jane had taken the risky step of asking the magistrate, Villienne, sole representative of the British Crown on the island and supposed enemy of all things piratical, for help. Though forbidden to go anywhere near the magistrate's mansion by her parents, Little Jane had ascended the hill to seek him out. It was a desperate gamble, but she could think of no one else with the medical skills needed to help her friend Ishiro, who had fallen gravely ill during their escape from the burning ship.

Little Jane had not passed through the magistrate's gates undisturbed, however. Her presence there aroused the ire of the two nastiest people in Smuggler's Bay, the wickedly well-bred, implacably evil twins Charity and Felicity. After narrowly avoiding exposure to hazardous waste at their horrid hands, she managed to find Magistrate Villienne at last, peacefully experimenting with volatile chemicals in his greenhouse laboratory. Unfortunately, the distraction of Little Jane's unexpected appearance led to an accidental explosion. Luckily, Villienne emerged from the disaster reasonably unharmed and, thankfully, still willing to help her. It was the only piece of good fortune she'd had all week.

Late that night, Little Jane returned to the Spyglass Inn with Harley, an old hand from the *Pieces of Eight* currently employed as Magistrate Villienne's butler.

She recognized the magistrate's tall, thin shadow at the windowpane and the odd accent that floated down to her from the open window. Villienne was already there.

Unfortunately, the tavern regulars had prevented him from going in to see Ishiro. Suspicion concerning magistrates ran high among the patrons of the Spyglass Inn and Tavern, most of whom were pirates, ex-convicts, or relatives of the same.

"I was told there was a man here —" protested the magistrate as Jane and Harley entered the establishment.

"Look, if you ain't wantin' something to wet yer whistle, ain't nothing fer you here. This here's a sailor's bar. Might as well be on yer way back to your proper place, eh?" Jonesy the bartender hefted a heavy keg of rum threateningly into position behind the bar. "Gettin' dark out. Wouldn't want to trip on your way back to your mansion, now would ya?"

Sucking in her fear and tucking in her shirttail, Little Jane entered the fray hoping Jonesy would listen to common sense for once. It was all rather ridiculous, she thought, considering Villienne's weedy, unprepossessing figure and the fact that his hair still stood straight up from his head, a lingering result of the explosion from the night before. He couldn't have looked more *un*magisterial.

"Very well, I know where I'm not wanted," confessed the magistrate, turning toward the door, shoulders slumped in defeat and humiliation. He was relieved to spy Little Jane's small frame by the light of the doorway. "You said there was a sick man for me to see," he whispered irritably.

"There is," she assured him. "Don't worry, I'll straighten them out."

"Jonesy, let the magistrate be," Little Jane advised her cousin. "He don't want to arrest anyone. Can't you see he's here to tend to Ishiro in his illness? The man's a doctor."

"Almost-doctor," Villienne corrected her nervously. "Never quite managed to graduate medical college. Couldn't stomach the surgery, you see." He shivered visibly at the recollection. "Don't you worry, though. Most likely it's not *that* sort of problem," Villienne added, by way of reassurance.

Jonesy narrowed his eyes skeptically at the magistrate. "Well, if you vouches for him, I guess it's all right," was all he said.

"Excellent!" Villienne rubbed his chemical-stained hands together. "Time's a wasting, my good man. Please, show me to him."

"Over here," said Little Jane, motioning for him to follow her. She guided Villienne to Ishiro's narrow, high-ceilinged chamber just off the room that housed the tavern.

Ishiro lay on his cot surrounded by towering stacks of drawing books, which Little Jane knew were filled with sketches from every year of his long life at sea. She watched anxiously as Villienne examined him. The magistrate *seemed* friendly enough so far, but she still didn't trust him. A man who employed the likes of Bertina, Charity, and Felicity as domestic help could easily turn evil by mere association.

Then there was the matter of his name — *Villienne*. He pronounced it *Vi-lain*, which sounded far too much like *villain* for her taste. Like most pirates, Little Jane put plenty of stock in names. Her own name, for instance, aggravated her deeply. She sincerely believed that if she could somehow get the ship's crew to stop calling her "Little Jane," she'd have an easier time earning their respect.

People's characters were supposed to match their names, she knew. It was the rule in all the plays she'd seen with her parents in London. Characters with names like Captain Sneerwell and Lady Rottenheart rarely revealed themselves to be nice, friendly chaps or ladies.

But the Haymarket Theatre was far away now, she mused, and there weren't many people left who she could ask for help. Everything she'd known her whole life and most everyone she'd counted on — her ship, her family, the crew — had vanished in a single day. Her parents couldn't help her now, not where they were — if they still *were* at all. It was a wonder the sun still rose in the east and set in the west, when everything else was so upside down. She stroked the wood grain on Melvin, the wooden practice sword her mother had given her, but it provided little comfort.

She still didn't know who'd ordered the *Panacea* to kidnap her parents and destroy their ship. Certainly, Villienne had a motive for doing it. As a magistrate, surely it was his job to turn their island of rebels and reprobates into a piracy-free colony of tax-paying citizens. Perhaps she'd made a grave error bringing him here.

Suddenly, she heard an old, tired sigh rise up from the bed. Ishiro had not said a word since they'd disembarked from the *Medusa*, the fishing boat that had rescued them from the fiery destruction of the *Pieces of Eight* four days earlier.

Little Jane thought Ishiro had gone off to sleep after the initial surprise of Villienne's appearance at his bedside, but no, he was awake, propped up on his elbows and speaking, though his voice sounded creakier and more heavily accented than usual.

"What's that?" he wheezed, struggling for breath.

Little Jane turned her face away, not wanting to see her friend brought so low. In Villienne's hand she saw a clear glass flask stopped up with cork. Shaking the contents lightly, he held the bottom of the flask over the candle flame. Inside, a cloudy green liquid bubbled to life.

"What's that?" Little Jane asked, curious despite herself.

"I've managed to distill this from a rather curious plant I extracted a few months ago from a rock behind the outhouse," Villienne explained. "I tested it on my tabby cat when he seemed poorly last month and it positively reinvigorated him. At any rate, it did until my man found him drifting by a fishermen's hut in a toy boat wearing a bonnet." Villienne frowned at the puzzling memory. "Poor puss, he just hasn't been right since. Climbs the bleeding curtains whenever Charity or Felicity set foot in the room. Very strange," he murmured, his eyes taking on a faraway look.

"You was saying?" interrupted Jonesy impatiently. He had followed them to the room and now stood leaning on the doorframe, brawny arms crossed.

"Ah, where was I? The plant, yes, a lichen actually," Villienne continued brightly. "Aside from this concoction here, I've managed to distill and compress the stuff into lovely little pellets. Care to try one?" With a flourish, Villienne produced from his pocket a greenish-brown pellet covered in a considerable amount of grey trouser lint.

"Uh, maybe another time," Little Jane said, wrinkling her nose.

Villienne looked expectantly to Jonesy, but the barkeeper just shook his head.

"Are you certain?" asked Villienne, crestfallen. "I think they could be a corking success if people would just try them. I've written letters to notable scientists back home trying to pique their interest, but no one ever writes back. I find it rather discourteous, to tell you the truth, and also curious, for I never seem to get any mail at all from England or the Continent anymore."

"No mail whatsoever?" asked Little Jane suspiciously.

The magistrate nodded. "Do you have any idea how long I've been pining for my *Linnaean Society Monthly Journal*? I only received Part 1 of 'The Lifecycle of Barnacles' and I've been in suspense for months wondering whether the creatures are hermaphrodites or not."

"By the by," Little Jane said conversationally, "I seen those twins, Charity and Felicity, making some very odd looking fires on the beach. Looked like some sort of natural history magazine."

"My articles!" The magistrate blanched.

"Ain't the first time," growled Jonesy, clenching his fists. "I ever catch them two pyros skulking round here again, I'll —"

"Let's return to the matter of this so-called pirate hunter — the *Panacea* you said it was called," said Villienne, trying to salvage what dignity he could. "I'd be a fool not to realize that every person on this island has a loved one on the *Pieces of Eight*. It is my responsibility to serve the *people* of this island, above all, and I say it was quite bad form for someone to take my citizens' ship by force! Personally, I believe violence is only the province of the impatient, the incompetent, and the seriously-out-of-options. And *I*, as you may well notice, am none of the above."

With that, Villienne uncorked the flask with a dramatic pop.

Little Jane cocked an eyebrow at the magistrate. For the life of her, she couldn't figure out whether he was completely brilliant or as mad as a box of frogs. But whichever it was, she was convinced Villienne hadn't been the one to hire the *Panacea* to hunt down her parents.

After stirring the mixture, Villienne doled out the precise amount for Ishiro with a hastily cleaned spoon provided by Jonesy.

Little Jane stared worriedly at the odd green pellets and strange liquid preparation. It was certainly a novel method of treatment, she'd give him that. But would it help Ishiro?

"What's wrong with trusty old leeches?" Jonesy asked suspiciously.

Ishiro swallowed the green liquid in one gulp. Little Jane watched carefully for signs of imminent poisoning.

"Bah!" Ishiro grimaced. "Jonesy, fetch me something to wash this down."

"You're lucky I had enough of it on hand," said Villienne to Little Jane. "If *somebody* hadn't caused me to blow up my laboratory, I might have had something to add to improve the taste."

"We think there might be something wrong with his heart," said Little Jane softly to Villienne. "It seems the pain is centred there."

"Hmmm … I believe you are correct. It seems he may have had a cardiac attack." Villienne frowned as Jonesy re-entered the room carrying a cup of sake, a bowl of chocolate, and what looked to be a side of beef, dripping with fat.

"Ishiro," said Villienne, "I suggest you desist in con-
suming alcoholic spirits and rich foods if you plan on
staying with us."

The magistrate turned to Jonesy, frowning. "You'll
make sure of that, won't you?"

"What?"

"Yes, sir," promised Little Jane in Jonesy's stead. "He
won't touch a drop. Then he'll be better again, right?"

Villienne looked into her small, worried face and
sighed, remembering why he'd chosen to forsake the medical profession. "I think he is doing considerably better
already, but any further stress on his heart muscle could
be fatal. He must have calm and sleep and plenty of this
mixture. Do you understand?"

"Yes."

"Now, Mr. Ishiro, it's time you got some rest. There's
nothing for healing quite like it," advised Villienne.

"Come on, old son, let me at least give you supper,"
Jonesy urged Villienne. "Shame to let a good steak go
to waste."

Villienne looked at the large, tattooed barkeep, wanting very much to go home instead.

"Thank you for the offer. Tomorrow, perhaps," he
suggested, "when I come back in the morning to see to
the patient."

Early the next morning Little Jane had a startlingly
vivid dream that her parents hadn't really been captured
and it was all just a complicated birthday surprise gone

awry. They were hiding with Jonesy behind the bar all along, like they did when she turned eight, ready to spring out with rum cakes and sugar cane drinks, shouting "surprise" when she appeared. Only she hadn't come and they'd been forced to eat the cakes themselves. She heard them talking about it from behind the screen that divided their side of the room from hers, expressing their disappointment.

She woke with a start and pushed the screen back, ready to explain to them what had happened. By the half-light of dawn, she blinked at their unslept-in sheets and remembered. She pulled her blanket tight around her shoulders and sat down in her mother's creaky rocking chair. A yellow square of early morning light moved gradually over their empty bedspread. Dust specks drifted in the stream of light, illuminating three abandoned shoes, still waiting patiently on the mat by the door.

"What would you have me do?" Little Jane implored them, but the shoes did not reply.

She sat and stared for a long time, thinking furiously, unable to come up with a single solution. Finally, the sound of Villienne's voice greeting Jonesy downstairs disrupted her reverie. She quickly got dressed and ran down to join them.

Villienne sat stiffly at the table while Jonesy and Harley stabbed enthusiastically at slabs of bloody beef. Little Jane couldn't help noticing how jumpy the magistrate was. Any second now he would find some pretext to bolt off to look in on Ishiro, and she hadn't had a chance to talk to him yet. She could not allow that. With every minute lost she was painfully aware the *Panacea* was sailing ever closer to its mysterious destination and ever farther away from Smuggler's Bay. She shuddered to think of it. Somebody had to do something, say something.

Finally, Little Jane put down her fork. "So, what's the plan?"

"What plan?" asked Harley.

"When're we going after the enemy? How do we find them? What's our strategy?"

"What're ye talking about?" asked Jonesy.

"The enemy — that ship, the *Panacea* — we have to go after them."

"We have no plan," replied Jonesy miserably.

"Then it's time we made one, inn'it?"

"Little Jane," Jonesy began, in one of those regretfully-explaining-the-harsh-nature-of-the-Real-World tones adults sometimes put on. "It ain't as simple as that."

"You just don't care because they're not yer parents!" she snapped.

"C'mon," said Jonesy, leaning down to look her in the eye, "I love Bonnie Mary and Jim like me own brother and sister, but that ain't gonna pay the rent on a ship or outfit her rig and hire on a crew. 'Sides which, who knows which way they gone? Like as not we'd be sailing for years trying to find 'em."

"Pirate hunters take their captives back with 'em to England to try 'em at Old Bailey, right?" Little Jane pressed him.

"Says who? They might make trial at any British port — Jamaica, St. Kitts, or Nevis. Who knows?"

"What's to assume they're even British to begin with?" added Villienne. "Did anyone here see what flag they flew?"

"Didn't get me a good look," confessed Little Jane, "but me dad said he saw the union jack a-flying as the ship approached."

"But if she's a pirate hunter, then that means they got permission from the Crown, a letter of marque and the like," added Harley gloomily. "Maybe even redcoats on board, who knows."

Little Jane felt her soul sink inside her at their reasonable arguments. It made her *furious*. These people had been doing foolish, unreasonable things for as long as she could remember. What gave them the right to suddenly turn sensible now?

"Fine! You lot just sit here on your cowardly wobble-bottoms then," cried Little Jane, rising abruptly from the table. "I'll go after them meself, I will."

"No, you won't," proclaimed a wheezy voice behind her. "I'm coming with you."

Her head whipped round, and she was shocked to see Ishiro standing there. "Ishiro, what're you doing? I thought you was sick?"

"I am," Ishiro said, his voice still weak, but growing steadier. "Still, it don't mean I ain't got a say in where I goes."

"Don't be daft, Ish," said Jonesy. "Going running after 'em half-cocked like this'll kill you certain."

"I'm afraid he's right, Mr. Ishiro. You'd be risking another heart attack," contended Villienne gravely. "I don't recommend —"

"I'd sooner die working the deck than lying in me bed like a bleedin' coward!" exclaimed Ishiro. "On any account, I'm much improved. Whatever you puts in that drink, it's better'n *sake*."

"But you're the cook," argued Villienne. "Begging your pardon, sir, but even I know that it takes more than a little culinary knowledge to command a sailing vessel."

"I'll have Little Jane here to help me," replied Ishiro. "Not to mention the fact that, like yourself, I am a man of many talents. Betting, for instance."

"Betting?"

"Aye, betting. For example, right now I'm willing to bet I know exactly where that other ship's taken 'em."

They all watched as Ishiro picked Jonesy's steak knife off the table and walked over to the dusty mirror hanging behind the bar. He slid the knife into a gap under the right corner of the frame, forcing the point in under the glass. With a grunt, he twisted the knife and the mirror gave way. The glass tumbled out of the frame and crashed to pieces on the floor.

"What in blazes did you do that for?" asked Jonesy. "Are you completely off your nut, Ish? That glass was still in good nick!"

It had taken Ishiro much effort to remove the glass in his current weakened state, but now he stood triumphant in front of the back of the frame, his purpose revealed. Stepping delicately over the broken pieces of glass on the floor, Little

Jane made her way to where he stood, ducking up under his arm so she could see what he saw. With a shaking hand, the cook pointed at the cardboard backing. Little Jane could just make out a picture there. It was a strange floating landscape painted with a black calligraphy brush. And she was certain that the hand that had painted it — his style still recognizable even after so many years — was that of Ishiro Soo-Yun.

But this was no simple landscape painting. Alongside it were pairs of numbers side by side — she recognized them from her mother's weekly navigation lessons as coordinates of longitude and latitude.

Little Jane smiled. She could read them. Two thumb widths west of Grand Cayman Island, right above where Ishiro's finger touched the picture, was a little dot of an island. Beside it, in tiny, careful print, she read the words *Nameless Land Mass.*

"The Nameless Isle," Little Jane whispered. Suddenly, it all made sense. "Of course, whoever took them would be wanting to go there. Some villain must've heard tell of the treasure. Ned! He'd be the man spreadin' it around, I wager."

"You couldn't 'ave just told us that without damaging the furnishings, eh?" complained Jonesy.

"Sorry, Mr. Jones. Flares of the dramatics, and all, I guess." Ishiro shrugged sheepishly.

"Ned knew the coordinates, too," said Little Jane with frustration. "It were his job to take the captains' instructions to the crew and make sure they was followed."

"We have to get to the island afore they do," added Ishiro firmly. "It's the only hope they got. Do you think Ned knows where the loot's hid?"

"Impossible! The coordinates of the island, *yes*, the location of the treasure, *never*," scoffed Little Jane. "Me parents weren't trusting him *that* far. They're the only ones what ever dared go."

"How clever," said Villienne excitedly, as if it were all the plot of some grand adventure story he'd just discovered. "The captains wouldn't have any from the crew follow them to the island, for fear of someone else discovering where they'd been hiding their ill-gotten gains all these years, is that right?"

Jonesy cocked an eyebrow at Villienne. "Ill-gotten gains? What's that supposed to mean?"

"Don't be ridiculous," said Little Jane. "It's because the island's cursed, that's all."

"Cursed?" asked Villienne.

"Everyone knows my parents were the only ones what ever survived a night on the isle. I ain't never seen no one else go there meself to test out the curse, but I think it still stands."

"But then, that's good," said Villienne.

"It's *good* that me parents was captured and forced to show this pirate hunter around a cursed island what might kill them?"

"No, it's good because whoever captured them will need the captains alive to make sure they lead them the right way to the treasure."

"Oh. I didn't think of that."

"I take it you and your parents are the only ones who know exactly where on the island the loot is hidden?" asked Villienne.

"No, only them," said Little Jane softly. "I was never told."

"Why didn't they tell you?" asked her cousin tactlessly. "That loot be *your* inheritance."

Why *hadn't* her parents trusted her with their secrets? She was their daughter and Ishiro was just a friend, after all. Why hadn't they bothered to tell her where they'd hidden their loot?

"And what about you now, Jonesy?" asked Ishiro shrewdly. "Ain't they told you? Yer blood relatives with Bonnie Mary. She say anything to you about where the loot's hid?"

"Uh … well, now that ye mention it, someone might've said somefing." Jonesy scratched his head.

"So why're you holdin' out on us, Jonesy?" asked Harley.

Suddenly, Jonesy seemed very preoccupied with polishing the spoon he'd lent to Villienne.

"Mr. Stevin Jones, your duty to the captains is clear," said Ishiro in a voice he'd last used years ago to urge reluctant men to battle. "I swear to you, their secret won't ever leave this room. Now tell us, where did Long John and Bonnie Mary hide it?"

"All right," Jonesy answered, in a barely audible voice. Little Jane had no idea her big, gruff cousin could make such a tiny sound. "They did tell me."

"And?" they all asked at once.

"And then …" Jonesy looked down. "I forgot."

"What?"

"They'd no business trusting me," he burst out. "They knew I were a brawler in me younger days. Little Jane, I'm sorry," Jonesy implored his cousin. "You *know* I was hit in the head so many times I can't even remember the words to 'Bottle of Rum' to save me life — and I've heard that song a thousand times. How'd they think I'd remember the code — a whole bunch of foreign words I ain't ever heard before?"

Little Jane gaped at her cousin. Even if by some miracle they managed to get a boat to the Nameless Isle, they'd never be able to locate the hidden cache of loot before the pirate hunters got to it. Not if the pirate hunters had her parents' knowledge and they had nothing.

This is it then, she thought. *We'll never win.* Her eyes spilled over with tears.

Seeing his little cousin cry so openly, Jonesy felt his own heart nearly crack in two. "So many times I been wanting to ask them to tell me again, but I were always too shamed to do it. I never meant to let them down, Jane. They gave me a chance, back when there weren't nobody else in the world what would. If there be anything I can do to fix this, I'll do it, I swear."

Jonesy looked so forlorn that she thought he might weep too. Little Jane reached out and squeezed his large, branded hand. "There are plenty o' maps in their room upstairs. One of them might be a map of the island. Don't matter if we have to look all over the island without the coordinates, we'll find them, I know we will!" she said, filling her voice up with as much confidence as she could muster. "Just get me to the island and I'll figure it out. Maybe they've left some clues there to lead us to them, who knows?" She looked around at the serious faces that surrounded her. "So, who's with me?"

Jonesy shook off his grief and placed his hand on her shoulder. "I suppose it beats sitting around here on our wobble-bottoms, as you said. Only thing is, how're we going to get us a ship?"

"We could steal one," suggested Harley.

"A whole ship? Don't be daft," Jonesy said.

"But you're pirates," Villienne commented, genuinely curious as to the reasons for their refusal. "Is that not what you do on a regular basis?"

"Actually, I *was* a pirate. I'm your butler now," Harley corrected his employer.

"And I'm just a barkeep with an unfortunate memory problem," added Jonesy.

"We prefer to be called *privateers*, not pirates, any-way," Little Jane commented.

"And most privateers are not complete idiots," sniffed Ishiro. "There's no port anywhere I can think of with a dock that ain't crawling with soldiers paid for nothing but the guarding of ships. It's a whole lot easier to steal a ship at sea where there's no one around to watch."

"So we got to rent us a ship then," suggested Jonesy.

"And for that we be needin' gold," said Harley.

"Hmmm," Ishiro muttered, deep in thought, "gold …"

Idly, Little Jane studied the map that had been hidden behind the mirror, wondering if it held any more clues. Her gaze came to rest on its frame. It was pewter work of a very old, ornate style with patches of gold. Suddenly, she had an idea.

"We could start by selling this picture frame. It might make us a *little* gold, don't you think?"

Jonesy scratched his head. "You know, now that you mention it, I do have a souvenir silver teaspoon from Brighton. Might be worth somefing."

"How about this gold watch?" offered Villienne, pulling a large watch on a chain from his pocket. "It doesn't actually work, but it really looks like it might, wouldn't you say?"

Little Jane looked thoughtfully at the watch. "You know, I think that might work."

"Oh, no." Villienne laughed. "I assure you, this watch is really quite broken."

"No, I mean this brilliant idea that just came to me. Jonesy, remember the time we went to that big market in Jamaica?"

"The one in Kingston?"

"Aye. Remember you was sayin' a fellow could sell anything there. *Anything*."

Her cousin grinned, finally beginning to catch her drift. "Anything that can be carted or carried or shipped or ferried. There's people there what'd buy *our* junk even."

Little Jane smiled back. They had a plan.

Captain Madsea no longer ventured into the *Panacea*'s stateroom to dine with the other officers these days. It had been a week at least since he'd last set foot on deck and yet another rumour was scurrying through the *Panacea*, fleet as a rat fleeing a sinking ship, that the captain might die any day.

Madsea lay abed in his stateroom, undergoing the patient ministrations of Doc Lewiston, his personal physician.

"Not the first time they've said that about me," observed the captain dryly, when informed of the talk going round.

Though it could be the last, thought Lewiston, worry corrugating his brow. He blew on a cup of medicinal tea and raised it to Madsea's cracked lips. The captain lifted his head weakly off the pillow, but made no motion to open his mouth.

"Come on, Captain, just a drop," Lewiston coaxed. "I put some rose hips in it that should clear those lungs right up."

"Fine, fine," rasped Madsea. "Long as you keep those filthy leeches off me."

Lewiston sheepishly nudged a wriggling basket of leeches under the bed with the toe of his boot, hoping the captain wouldn't spot them.

"Did he eat anything for breakfast?" Lewiston asked the steward, Darsa.

"A bite or two of eel pancake, sir," replied the young man, with a nervous glance at the fireplace where Doc Lewiston was busy tapping out the ashes of his pipe. Darsa was right to be nervous. Soon Lewiston noticed the hastily hidden wad of blood-speckled handkerchiefs wedged under the unlit coals.

Upon closer inspection, Lewiston noticed more handkerchiefs on the floor that hadn't even made it the short distance to the fireplace. Doc Lewiston frowned. He always knew things were getting bad when the captain started losing his aim.

"What's all this?" asked Lewiston accusingly, holding one up with the end of the fire poker.

"I thought I told you to clean this place up," Captain Madsea hissed at the hapless Darsa.

"Sorry, Capt'n," muttered the steward as he grabbed a broom.

With a sigh, Lewiston lit the fire and watched it consume the much-abused handkerchiefs. Darsa left as quickly as he could.

"You must listen to me, Fetzcaro," insisted Lewiston once Darsa had left. He was taking unusual liberty in using the captain's first name, but Lewiston knew if he didn't get the stubborn man's attention somehow his captain would soon be dead. "This over-exertion must stop. Your health can't take much more. You mark my words; it'll kill you if you continue."

"It makes no difference. I'll die anyway," said Madsea, resigned. "As long as I live long enough to mete out the punishment those two blackguards deserve and to reclaim the bounty that is rightfully mine, I'll go to me maker in peace."

"You see," groaned Lewiston with mounting frustration, "that's it right there. That's the problem — your preoccupation with this fabled treasure. It's preposterous. What sort of pirate saves up twenty years' worth of loot anyway? I've been a physician to navies and sailors half my life and if there's one thing I know, it's that there's nobody better at losing money in a hurry than your average seaman. And pirates are the worst of the wicked lot! Providence! Even Admiral Collingwood himself was known to blow an entire month's pay packet on powdered wigs in less than an hour. Not to mention Lord Nelson and his silverware collection. And these were respectable men, heroes to the nation even. If you had an ounce of sense, Captain, you'd know that every single penny those pirates ever made is long gone, spent lining the pockets of tavern keepers from Calais to Cape Town. This legend of a cache of gold is nothing but a fool's fantasy."

"And I would agree with you on all points if we were talking about your ordinary, average pirate. But not these two, Lewy. I know these scoundrels inside and out. Seamen of a most irregular sort, Bright and Silver are — schemers, master-plotters, cunning deceivers, and hoarders most foul. You mark my words; I'd wager they've been laying up that treasure on the island for years. Just ask that man Ronk from their ship. He'll attest to it."

Doc Lewiston shook his head. "You're risking everything on the word of one man. And him a traitor to his own captain at that! How do you expect to go tramping around some godforsaken tropical island in the middle of flaming nowhere looking for some hypothetical treasure anyway, when you can barely lift your head off the pillow?"

"I shall be serviceable by the time we reach the island," said Madsea firmly. "*You* will see to *that*."

"Then you have far more confidence in my abilities than I do." Lewiston snorted.

"The will can be quite a powerful instrument, my medical friend, and I *will* find that treasure, you'll see." Madsea's words were bold, and even with his voice so ragged, there was ironclad determination in every syllable.

He just might at that, thought Lewiston. He couldn't help but admire the man's tenacity.

But then Madsea sank back down on his pillow, seemingly as weak as ever.

"*Mad*-sea," said Lewiston. "You're an aptly named captain at that, you know."

"Oh, I do," replied Madsea, a mocking smile briefly pulling at the corners of his lips.

It wasn't long before word spread throughout Smuggler's Bay about the Great Sale. People trekked down to the Spyglass from near and far (and in the case of Smuggler's Bay, "far" was a maximum of two miles away) to offer up their valuables to help fund the effort to rescue the crew of the *Pieces of Eight*.

They'd collected a motley assortment of objects; some had no monetary value whatsoever, but Little Jane hadn't the heart to reject anything freely given. The people of the Bay didn't have much, but for the rescue fund they might need it all. Every dented tin cup, blunt carving knife, and water-damaged book was welcome in the pile of things to be sold at the great market in Kingston.

Little Jane witnessed a family with but a single plate in their possession lay that treasured item reverently down upon the pile like an offering. Little Jane was ashamed to take such a precious family heirloom, but she did. Despite being a pirate's daughter, Little Jane had never really been particularly greedy or gold-crazy. However, her parents' predicament seemed to have activated whatever latent portion of avarice lay slumbering within her, and so she took what they gave, no questions asked, and she was greatly moved by their generosity. The sale of such precious objects was a lot to knowingly entrust to a group of professional thieves, she had to admit, but then, except for Villienne, everyone on the island had *someone* they cared about on the *Pieces of Eight*.

Soon all the little boats of the island, along with the Hallbrooks' fishing vessel (Captain Hallbrook had generously offered to escort the rest of them back to his hometown of Kingston), were marshalled into a little convoy, prepared to set sail.

Little Jane hefted her kit bag onto her shoulder as she took one last look around the Spyglass. Little that could be physically moved had survived the merciless culling. Even the tables and chairs were gone. She noticed a mug still resting on the bar and snagged that, too. Clutching the mug tight to her chest, she took one last look around, wondering if she would ever be back.

At least some good had come of the captain's resurgent illness. Without Madsea to stop him, Doc Lewiston now had free reign over the two pirate captains in the brig. This was pleasant news indeed to Long John and Bonnie Mary, who had been working on Lewiston all week to let them up on deck for a breath of fresh air.

The good doctor agreed that a turn outside would do them good and so he procured the services of two sturdy sailors with two equally sturdy lengths of rope to serve as pirate-walkers.

As humiliating as it is to be walked like a dog in front of one's former crew members, after a week in the wretched environs of the brig the captains were ecstatic to be anyplace at all where they could actually feel the sun on their faces. They stood on deck blinking like a pair of moles, dazzled by the unaccustomed brilliance. Bonnie Mary sucked in a great lungful of fresh ocean air, and as the *Panacea* rolled gently to port, she felt the familiar spray of salt water on her cheek like a cleansing caress.

Long John shifted awkwardly with the ship's motion, unaccustomed to the crutches the doctor had given him.

"You all right there, Silver?" asked Doc Lewiston.

"Right as rain, me good man," Long John replied, feeling good to be up and about on the deck of a ship again, even if it wasn't his own. As he watched the gulls wheeling above the mainmast and the men scampering up the ratlines, any cobwebs still left clinging to his mind from his time in the brig blew out to sea. His senses felt fresh as a new coat of paint.

Upon seeing his former crewman Lockheed sitting by the mizzenmast with his back to the sail, busy splicing a line, Long John tugged on his leash, angling for a chat.

Bonnie Mary's mood darkened as she watched the warm exchange of pleasantries between Long John and the group of crewmen from the former *Pieces of Eight*.

Talkative and showy as always, she thought, shaking her head. Any advice about keeping a low profile had clearly gone in one ear and out the other. What was it her father always said at times like this? It'll all end in bloodshed. And he was usually right, at that.

What did Jim have to be so cheery about anyway? They were *this* close to death and here he was jawing away with the crew like they were back at the Spyglass and not on the deck of an enemy ship with a few inches of timber separating them from someone whose greatest desire in life was to kill them both, preferably in the most painful way possible.

She resigned herself to being the one, once again, to work out the logistical details of yet another of her husband's crazy plans. But it was a relief to see him smile again, at any rate. What was the other thing her father always said? If you can't beat 'em, join 'em.

The plan could wait for the moment. All she really wanted to think about for a few seconds was the liberating feel of the west wind in her hair. So she headed up to the waist of the ship to join Jim, letting the sailor holding the other end of her "leash" trail after her.

Weaponsmaster Jezebel Mendoza looked up from picking oakum to see Captain Bonnie Mary Bright being led by a huge bearded sailor across the deck.

"Captain," Mendoza said, rising with a reverent salute to her superior officer.

Bonnie Mary smiled graciously and saluted her in return.

"Captain Bright," piped up young Rufus, the cabin boy, who stood at her back. This was followed by salutes from Lockheed and Lancashire. Bonnie Mary smiled at this, for no one had ever bothered to salute the captains back on the *Pieces*. It seemed too elitist a gesture by far on a pirate ship where they each had equal vote. But here, in this hostile place, it was a sign that they still flew the black flag of the *Pieces* in their hearts, even though the ship herself was gone.

"Ahoy now! Stop that!" cried the guard, yanking on the rope and nearly knocking her off her feet.

Dvorjack and Changez joined Lancashire, Rufus, and Mendoza in shooting the guard some sinister looks. It escaped no one's notice that at the end of the hempen rope Dvorjack had just finished coiling was a four-pronged metal grappling hook of menacing appearance. The burly former purser of the *Pieces of Eight* held it now, tapping it against his hand, as if contemplating whether to swing it at Bonnie Mary's guard. In a split second, the ship's waist was crowded with the *Panacea*'s small contingent of riflemen, bristling with bayoneted weapons. The moment passed without any action being taken.

Only weaponsmaster Mendoza seemed uncowed by this sudden show of force.

"Phonies," she sniffed, to no one in particular. "Why, if those rifles aren't cheap, knock-off replicas, I'll eat my hat. Who ever heard of a *Backer* rifle? A standard issue rifle ought to be a Baker — *B-A-K-E-R*. Are your officers illiterate or simply incompetent? And you call yourselves fighters." She shook her head in disbelief. "For shame."

The riflemen — most of who could not, in fact, read — examined their weapons in confusion.

"Doc Lewiston," thundered Jesper, first officer of the *Panacea* (who *could* read, but much to his embarrassment had never noticed the name on his firearm). "What in the world do you think you're doing, allowing the prisoners to fraternize in this way? Did the captain give his permission for this?"

"You two," Jesper yelled to the guards. "Take those prisoners back to the brig. They're not to be let out for anything, do you understand? You may be in charge of a surgery in Suffolk, Doctor, but you ain't charged with command of this ship."

"And would somebody shut that skirt up!" Jesper pointed at Jezebel Mendoza. "Since when did a woman know anything about weapons anyway? A female weaponsmaster. What a joke."

But despite this bluff and hearty show, Jesper groaned as he watched the guards escort the prisoners back to the brig. How could he have gone this long on board without realizing their weapons were knockoffs?

Bonnie Mary had just lowered her head to duck back down into the evil-smelling hold when she heard an unmistakable sound. Even before she looked up, her heart leapt for joy. Circling overhead, flapping its stubby wings like a frenzied windmill was an utterly ridiculous-looking bird. And it was wonderfully, brilliantly, incandescently *orange*.

Bonnie Mary caught Jim's eye as the guards shoved them back through the hatch, and saw her joy mirrored in his glance. They knew what the cry of the peculiar orange bird meant. The Nameless Isle was close.

The Hallbrooks' fishing boat, *Medusa*, arrived in Kingston the next morning, followed shortly by the smaller fishing boats of the citizens of Smuggler's Bay.

Little Jane had spent the entire voyage in a whirl of worry. She paced the *Medusa*'s deck thinking of every horrible calamity that might befall their little convoy until she was certain all the boats would end up sunk, taking all the islanders' valuables down with them. Eight-year-old Wayne Hallbrook followed her around, imitating her pace and trying to whistle. He was some comfort, it was true, but the tension didn't leave her until every last object from Smuggler's Bay was removed from the boats and laid out at the market.

Unloading everything was backbreaking work, but with many hands working together they managed to move it all out to the market in preparation for the big sale.

Once they were finished, Little Jane turned to the Hallbrooks.

"Thankee," she said solemnly to the captain and his son. "We wouldn't have survived without you." She handed Wayne the little bottle of green lichen salve Villienne had prepared for her. "Fer your mum," she said. "It might help with her cough."

"Godspeed to yah all," replied Captain Hallbrook. He and Wayne waved as they headed back out to sea and homeward. "Remember, Little Jane, yah always got a birth on the *Medusa* should yah ever need one."

Before the sailors of the *Panacea* knew quite what was happening, the peculiar orange birds had perched on every conceivable surface of the ship from the bowsprit to the forecastle. Much to the deckhands' annoyance, they then proceeded to soil the newly cleaned deck in multiple bursts of spontaneous defecation.

However, once the crew realized the obnoxious birds were not some new species of albatross (a bird that was considered exceedingly bad luck to kill), but instead resembled giant pigeons that had been crossed with flamingos, they primed the ship's kitchens for a feast.

Tovaliov, the *Panacea*'s cook, soon had the birds plucked of their orange feathers and mashed up into a delectable stew. There was plenty to go around, but the men of the *Panacea* made it a point not to share a single morsel with the captive crew of the *Pieces of Eight*. The *Panacea*'s men gorged themselves on second and third helpings of the delectable stew, gnawing on wings, legs, breasts, and gizzards, while the prisoners from the *Pieces* ate hard, weevily ship's biscuit without a word of complaint. Occasionally, the captives would share a dark look as their foes ate. A word was whispered softly among them and that word was *soon*.

As the market began to wind down, Little Jane set out to look for Jonesy. She discovered him holding court amid the remains of her father's mug collection, trying to palm off the last few pieces on a group of men from Trinidad.

"Jonesy!" She waved to her cousin and held up the drink she'd fetched for him from the beer tent before it closed down for the day. The sun was sinking, but the shadeless market still felt as hot as ever. Jonesy mopped his shining bald pate with his handkerchief as he accepted the cup of brew. Using his momentary distraction to their advantage, his prospective customers made themselves scarce.

Jonesy turned back to the rapidly emptying marketplace with a tired sigh. "I'm knackered. Where's that magistrate of yours?"

At the mention of his name, Villienne popped out of a cavernous chest clutching a blue and yellow striped parasol Little Jane hadn't used since she was six.

"Cheers all!" he said, twirling the parasol experimentally in his hands. The blue and yellow stripes blended to form a single uniform green as he spun the canopy before them.

"Can you believe some foolish person would actually part with such a superb demonstration of colour optics?"

Little Jane blushed.

Ishiro appeared soon after, looking exhausted. "I think we've done all we can," he said. "What's the score?"

"It can't be time to count up yet," pleaded Little Jane. "Look, the market ain't done. Surely, more people'll come."

"I don't think the rest o' this is going anywhere," said Jonesy with a wave of his hand at the mug collection. "C'mon, let's tally up."

Villienne spread out the day's takings.

Jonesy and Villienne both came up with the same sum in the end. Although it seemed like a great deal of money to Little Jane, neither of the adults looked happy.

"It ain't enough," complained Ishiro. "Not to get a boat, hire a crew and captain all."

"Is there anything more we can sell?" asked Little Jane hopefully.

"Everyfing's gone, love." Jonesy scuffed his shoes disconsolately in the dirt. Little Jane noticed they were missing the brass buckles they'd had the night before. If Jonesy was down to selling his shoe buckles, she knew the situation was even direr than she'd supposed.

"Nothing for it. We'll go to the shipwright tomorrow and see what he's willing to give us," she said resolutely.

What the clerk at Truthful Jack's Honest Shipyard showed them for their trouble the next morning was a longboat last used in the Napoleonic Wars. Its scuppers were clogged with decomposing leaves and its sails hung down from the masts in patchy rags.

"Leastways she's a hardy vessel," announced Harley hopefully, giving the mizzenmast a gentle thump. It split straight down the middle in response and conked him on the head. "Blast!" He rubbed the growing bump on his skull.

"Uh, I'll just go get Truthful Jack," mumbled the shipyard clerk as he ran off.

"This won't do," Ishiro scoffed. "No crew of mine'll sail the ocean in this."

Little Jane looked to Villienne. The magistrate fingered the official royal seal that hung around his neck, his habit whenever he was vexed by a particularly intractable problem. He rubbed his thumb over the relief of Lady Britannia in her helmet, but no inspired solution came to him.

"What's that?" asked Little Jane, pointing hopefully at the royal seal. "That might fetch a pretty penny if we were to sell it."

"What? This? Oh no, Little Jane, this isn't mine to sell. It's my badge of office and property of the Crown," Villienne explained proudly.

"But what do you use it for?"

"Oh, you know, sealing government documents for the British colonial office, letters to my mother, official reports, and —" Villienne stopped in mid-sentence. "Wait a tic. Someone give me a sheet of paper."

Ishiro obliged him with a page he tore from one of his drawing books. Villienne borrowed a pen from the ship-wright's writing desk, and scrawled something on the paper.

"What're ye doing?" asked Little Jane.

"Just requisitioning a ship for the Crown," replied Villienne airily as he continued writing.

Little Jane peered down at the writing on the paper. This is what it said:

> His Majesty, acting on behalf of the Colonial Affairs Office of the West Indies, hereby requests the use of your best ship in order to catch ~~criminary crossing error~~ an outlaw hateful to British interests in the West Indian colonies. If you comply with our most gracious request, mention of your most generous deed shall enter into our halls of power. We will make sure your great service to our interests is duly noted and you are awarded with a ~~crying horror~~ ...

There was more to the letter, further flattering prose, complete with vague allusions to some kind of reward from the Colonial Office that Little Jane was pretty sure did not exist.

"What's this part?" asked Ishiro, peering hard at the smeared passages in the document.

"Smudges," answered Villienne. "Let's just hope he doesn't ask. I couldn't write a fake name, sign it with the seal, and stay honest. I'm willing to do this to save lives, but I can still only stretch the truth so much in my position."

"You can take a ship just like that?" asked Little Jane, incredulous.

"Not take it, per say. Just sort of borrow it for a specific time," replied Villienne, uneasily. "Assuming this ruse works, of course."

"Of course."

Villienne then removed a stick of wax from his pocket. "Little Jane, fetch me a candle from my bag." Once he had lit the candle, he melted the wax down, letting it drip onto the paper. And finally, with a flourish he impressed the seal into the wax, rendering the document an official bequest of the British Crown.

"What's this then?" asked Greasy Barnard, the half-honest (if slightly greasy) half-brother of the completely dishonest (and non-greasy) Truthful Jack. "Ain't the longboat good enough fer you folk now?"

"I believe there's been a misunderstanding between us, my good man," replied Villienne, sounding every inch the well-turned-out gentleman, despite his raggedy clothes and messy hands, as he tried to explain the situation. Still, Greasy Barnard appeared unmoved, his arms crossed over his massive chest. He had barely blinked when Villienne broke the wax seal of the "official" document in front of him with a dramatic flourish.

"I ain't gots me specs and me brother ain't here," grumbled Barnard, scrutinizing the paper with narrowed eyes. His gaze jumped suspiciously from one word to another, and Little Jane rightly ascertained that he couldn't read even one of them. "Maybe you oughtta wait till Truthful Jack comes back —"

"I certainly will not!" yelled Villienne. "To lose further time would be a most regrettable disservice to His Majesty's Navy! In fact, I lose valuable time in discourse with you here now. Come, sir, I give my word as a gentleman that, as per the articles of the Van Hemphlin Agreement, I shall have your ship back to you in a fortnight. Should this offer fail to suit you, Mr. Barnard, I shall take my complaint up with the governor of Jamaica. Perhaps he will see your shipyard shut down for the foreseeable future. *Vous comprendez?*"

"What's that again?" Barnard asked nervously as he de-waxed his ear with the tip of his finger. Villienne patiently explained himself once more, until the man was nodding in agreement.

"Oh, yes, certainly, certainly, Yer Magistrateship. Fergive me. Come along. I got a fine ship o'the line, might well suit ya, kitted out with all the cannons an admiral might want. She ain't got a full job of paint on 'er yet, nor figurehead neither, but if'n you're not choosy…."

"That'll be fine," answered Villienne stiffly. All this lying was beginning to grate on his fundamentally honest nature.

Ishiro and Jonesy stared open-mouthed at the fine modern sloop Villienne had procured for them. The hull incorporated the new American innovation of live oak planking that was supposed to render a ship nearly cannon-proof. She was in the shipwright's dry dock now, just having her first coat of paint applied.

"Told ye he'd come in handy," was all Little Jane had to say.

A few hours later, their newly commandeered, half-painted ship was pulled out to the Kingston docks. It was quite a sight to see the ship splash down into the harbour. It reminded Little Jane of a duckling taking its first leap into a big pond; only in this case the "duckling" was as big as a whale.

Little Jane watched Villienne busying himself trying to scrape a promising looking barnacle off the underside of the dock and into one of his many specimen jars, oblivious to the massive ship being lowered down right next to him.

She couldn't quite believe what this man had just done for her and her family.

"Thank you so much for this," she said softly to him. "Don't matter what happens next, me and my family are in your debt forever, understand? I may be a different sort t'you, sir, but a Silver's word is her bond. Whatever help any of us can ever offer you, you just say the word, aye?"

"Aye?" answered Villienne.

"Aye." She winked back at him as he finally pried his barnacle loose.

"Didn't think you had it in you!" Jonesy slapped Villienne on the back, causing him to nearly drop the tiny creature. "Why, Long John himself woulda been hard-pressed to come up with anything better!"

"Please, I deserve no praise," confessed the magistrate shyly as he closed the lid of his specimen jar. "I just wanted to help."

"All well and good, but we still don't have supplies nor crew for her," announced Ishiro, bringing everyone back to reality.

"Ah, that." Little Jane sighed.

The supplies were the easy part. A sail to the Nameless Isle from Jamaica would only take two days if the weather held and then another two days back. They could use the money they made at the market to purchase what items they needed for such a short journey, but for the life of her, Little Jane had no idea how to go about finding crewmembers.

The original crew of the *Pieces of Eight* had come primarily from Smuggler's Bay and consisted of nearly all the able seamen of the village. The only ones who stayed behind when the *Pieces* sailed were a few fishermen. Two elderly fishermen who'd helped ferry the goods to Jamaica in their boats were willing to come aboard to help rescue their loved ones, but the rest of the crew, Little Jane realized with growing dismay, would have to be recruited from the dockside taverns of Kingston.

Chapter Two

Tale of an Atoll

In the brig of the *Panacea* "Long John" Jim Silver turned his face toward the tiny cross-hatched square of blue sky, eager to catch whatever whiff he could of the Nameless Isle on the air.

Though it lifted Long John's spirits, the volcanic scent of the approaching island only seemed to increase Bonnie Mary's fretful mood. As awful as their imprisonment was, it was trumped by the uncertain future awaiting them on the island.

Bonnie Mary originally assumed Fetz would leave Long John behind when they went ashore. After all, a man on crutches couldn't help but slow their party down, and the longer they remained on-island, the greater the risk to them all.

It would've been the logical decision. But logic, she now realized, held little sway over the mind of the captain.

Despite repeated arguments put forward by the good doctor, Madsea held fast to the belief that leaving Jim on board might court mutiny among the captive crewmembers. For her part, Bonnie Mary suspected another reason for Fetz's eagerness to take Jim, one she dared not voice aloud.

In her mind, Bonnie Mary ran through what she knew of the peculiar geography of the Nameless Isle: It was the type of volcanic island known as an atoll. At the centre of the island rose a tall mountain, the creation of a now dormant volcano, its surface pockmarked with caves created by lava flows thousand of years before. The passages through which the molten lava had once flowed formed tunnels that radiated from the centre of the volcano out to the surface. With the passage of time and the settling of the earth, the tubes had collapsed in on themselves and created the network of caves that now dotted the sloping sides of the mountain. No hiding place could be safer.

In addition, the mountain was surrounded on all sides by a wide ring of ocean water, like the moat around a castle. Around this moat was a circle of sharp basalt rocks that projected out of the ocean like an open mouth of crooked black teeth. The visible rocks were treacherous enough, but the ones to really watch out for were those hidden beneath the surface of the water, lying in wait for any ship foolish enough to sail too close.

A mantle of unseasonable fog had settled into the area as they approached. It rolled up over the ship, surrounding the *Panacea* in a shroud of white mist. Luckily, Madsea had sent out a small craft to take depth measurements, so they did not have to rely on sight alone for navigation.

Even so, it was a chancy manoeuvre. As the ship neared the black rocks, everyone braced for the inevitable crunch.

But thankfully no crunch came.

"Anchor dropped," came the call.

As the last of the anchor chain clanked off the spool, the curtain of fog parted and the Nameless Isle revealed itself in its entirety at last. It lay like some misty vision from a poet's dream, with the mountain rising up an eerie blue in the distance. Halfway up it vanished in a low wreath of cloud, only to emerge again on the other side, soaring to even greater heights before disappearing completely among the proper clouds of the sky.

It was the sort of vision that could take a person's breath away, but down in the brig, Bonnie Mary saw nothing save wood walls and iron bars.

With mounting terror, she wondered what fate Fetz had in mind for her and her husband. She was certain the real reason Jim was chosen for the journey was so that he could witness in person the destruction of all he'd loved and worked for during the years of Madsea's exile in prison.

Although they'd held out hope that Madsea would remain unaware of the general location of their loot on the island, somehow Ned had pieced together enough from overheard conversations during his time aboard to inform his new captain of the island's cave network as a likely spot.

Still, she was certain Madsea had no idea what they planned for him in return. Bonnie Mary had never taken the route they would tell Madsea to take to the cave. As far as she knew, no one ever had. In theory it should take them there, but she had no proof that it was even possible.

At least if they died on the journey, they'd take Fetz with them, she reasoned, but that was no comfort to her. All Bonnie Mary could think of was how terribly she missed Little Jane and how her arms ached to hold her. To risk her life travelling to the Nameless Isle was not the worst of it. The worst was that she still did not know where Little Jane was, whether she fared well or poorly, was safe or in danger. She had no idea whether Little Jane was even still alive, and to Bonnie Mary's mind no torture of body Madsea could ever inflict upon her could compete with the pain of not knowing that one simple fact.

Chapter Three

Captain Ishiro

If Jonesy, Ishiro, or Harley had any qualms about taking a twelve-year-old girl on a tour of dockside sailors' taverns in Kingston, they did not express them.

Truth was, the three men had so long been used to seeing Little Jane at the Spyglass that they had quite forgotten that another watering hole might not be so convivial to the young sailor girl, nor provide quite as wholesome an environment for her edification. As for Little Jane herself, she was entirely aware of her parents' prohibition toward such, but with them absent at the moment, she found no occasion to enlighten her friends about the rules she was breaking.

"Why in the world would anyone *want* to go inside one of these places?" Little Jane asked Jonesy, wrinkling up her nose upon entering a bar known locally as "The Chamber Pot."

Jonesy made no comment. He was too busy thumping on a table with his beefy fist, calling the drunken patrons to attention.

"Listen up, seadogs!" Jonesy's voice rang out above the general hubbub of the tavern. "Any sailor here looking to sign articles, we's seeking a crew for a few weeks' jaunt in the islands."

"What ship?" asked a curly-haired sailor with a red-veined nose.

"Truthful Jack's new sloop," answered Jonesy. "Straight out of the stocks she is, with the paint not even dry upon 'er. So, who here's got the spirit to join us?"

"A week's jaunt t' where?" piped up a grizzled seaman at the bar.

"Uh, yes, well, our destination be the Nameless Isle," replied Jonesy, nervously readjusting his neckerchief.

A buzz of whispered conversation sped around the room.

"The Nameless Isle?" asked a heavily freckled man, as if he hadn't heard quite right.

"The Cursed Isle, you mean," said another, spitting into a nearby cuspidor.

"Ain't it bewitched?" asked someone else.

"No, it ain't," replied Jonesy defensively.

"Aye," added Harley, trying to be helpful, "It's just a rumour. No one's been killed there in a dog's age."

Jonesy shot the ex-butler a look that could've withered wet grass. Luckily, he was distracted by yet another grizzled seaman (this particular bar did indeed seem to be lousy with them). The man squinted at Jonesy like he was a bit of irritating sun in his eyes.

"If ye were Long John Silver yerself, I wouldn't go with ye, ye was going *there*," he pronounced querulously, taking another swig of his brew as if to say *that* was the end of *that*.

"Here! Here!" agreed several others.

"Listen," cut in Ishiro before they all got back to their beers. "We're on a rescue mission to get back the crew of the *Pieces of Eight*, kidnapped less than a fortnight ago by pirate hunters and the ship sunk out from under them. You may see some action, but you'll be paid well and no one'll make you set foot on the island, I promise you that. Ask anyone here, they'll tell you Ishiro Soo-Yun's a man of honour. You sign on with us, I'll see to it personally that you'll get half your wages right now, *a-fore* we leave Jamaica."

This strange offer, accompanied by the news of the *Pieces'* destruction, set tongues wagging again.

"And who're you, Chinaman?" snorted the red-faced sailor.

"Actually, I'm half Korean, half Japanese," replied Ishiro, a fact that he had grown quite tired of repeating during his long life in Western lands.

"What business it be to you where he's from?" growled Little Jane. "He's our captain, so you best not get on the wrong side of 'im."

"Jane!" gasped Ishiro, feeling his heart jig up and down in his chest in a most unwelcome manner. "You know I can't captain a ship." But his voice was drowned out in a flurry of renewed conversation.

"That's right. Captain Ishiro!" Little Jane shouted. "The hero of the *Newton* and the *Golden Fleece*. Him what

brought three hundred men out of hell after the death o'
Old Captain Thomas Bright all them years ago. This be a
once-in-a-lifetime chance to serve under a decorated war
hero, or are you all so cowardly and shy of glory?"

All eyes in the tavern were now on the young girl.

"And who might you be, missy?" asked the bleary-
eyed sailor. He leaned forward menacingly, and she could
smell his sour breath on her face. "Nought but a wee lass
in pants, says I."

"I'm Little Ja — No, I mean, I'm Jane, Jane Silver. My
parents are the kidnapped captains of the —"

"Har har har." The bleary-eyed sailor drowned out
her voice with his laugh. "*Little* Jane? Wot kinda name
is that?"

"*She* better not be coming aboard," snorted the seaman with the red nose.

"Females is bad luck on a ship," growled another.

"Aye, mates, remember the tale of the chap what
brought his lass aboard the *Makanaw Mermaid* off
Boston. Ship sunk not a day later wit' all hands aboard,"
said an ancient white-haired mariner, busy holding court
in a corner of the tavern.

"Belay that talk and shut yer gobs!" shouted Jonesy
above them all, but his bluster was to no avail. The noise
from the crowd rose like flood water above their ears, sub-
merging all Little Jane and her friends tried to say beneath it.

Ishiro's chest was still too weak from his recent heart
trouble to make much of a dent in the din and Jonesy's voice
was rapidly going hoarse. Villienne was too stunned by his
unaccustomedly filthy surroundings to think of anything

except issues of infection control, and as for Harley, he was rapidly coming around to the tavern patrons' way of thinking about their expedition's chances for success.

Little Jane's face flushed and her cheeks glowed red as pokers in a fire. An onlooker might be mistaken in thinking she was blushing, embarrassed by the sailors' rough talk, but Little Jane wasn't embarrassed; no, Little Jane was *mad*. Mad in both senses of the word. Furious with the constant frustration and humiliation, harried to exhaustion by fear, and touched with just a bit of pure crazy for good measure.

Like the accidental mixture of chemicals in Villienne's greenhouse laboratory, something strange was bubbling up within her. Her emotions came swirling together in such high concentrations that they catalyzed into a runaway reaction of powerful unstoppability. Then, much like the chemicals in Villienne's greenhouse, Little Jane exploded.

"Enough!" she shouted, in a voice that travelled out of the bar, all the way down the street, and back again, loud as the sound of a cannon.

Propelled by a fury like none she'd ever felt before, Little Jane leapt up on the nearest table, sending the beer mugs flying.

"Quieeeettttttt!" she roared at the top of her lungs. And before she knew quite what was happening, the entire tavern fell silent, dumbfounded by the booming shout and its impossibly small source.

Even Little Jane herself couldn't quite fathom how that shout came to be. It was the kind of bellowing, deep throated shout that comes direct from the belly; the kind of shout that could command a crew over the raging winds of a hurricane; the kind of shout, in fact, that is usually only heard from the mouth of a genuine, full-grown ship's captain.

Just how such a shout came full throttle from the throat of the twelve year old girl in their midst no one could ever say, yet from that day forward Little Jane always knew that mighty shout was there, coiled like a sleeping dragon deep down inside her, a great power to be called forth whenever she truly needed it.

In the stunned silence of the dingy room her voice rang out loud and clear as she said, "Yes, I am a girl in pants." (No one even sniggered now). "But I'm also the daughter of Captains Bonnie Mary Bright and Long John Silver — and a bleedin' fine sailor to boot! I ain't afraid of the Nameless Isle and I'm younger'n all a you. C'mon, you lot. You call yourselves seadogs? What man among you ain't afraid of his shadow?" She laughed scornfully. "In fact, I'm so *not* afraid o' what's on that island that I ain't bringing nothing with me but me wooden sword here. It ain't worth me steel and neither is you!" She sniffed, cinched her mother's old red sash about her waist as if that was that, and stepped down lightly off the table. All eyes in the tavern followed her to the doorway, but she would not favour them with so much as a backward glance.

"And you say we gets half-pay before the ship even leaves harbour?" a voice piped up.

"Aye," answered Ishiro, his voice and manner invigorated by Little Jane's call to arms. "So make your choices wisely, mates, and sail with us."

All told, fifteen men signed articles for the *Yorkman* in that tavern alone.

Despite their success in recruiting a crew, by the time the group from Smuggler's Bay had returned to their camp at the marketplace, Ishiro had resumed his troubled countenance.

"It was wrong and you know it," argued the aggrieved sea cook as he paced in front of the fire. "I ain't captain material no more. And to bring up the *Newton* and the *Fleece* like that — what were you thinking?"

Little Jane twisted a braid nervously around her finger. Her stroke of genius in volunteering Ishiro for the captaincy without first asking his permission didn't seem like such a good idea anymore. She looked down, wishing she could just shout Ishiro into her way of thinking like she had the men at the tavern, but she knew he was one man whose decisions could never be swayed by the power of a mere voice, no matter how loud.

"It ain't as if the Admiralty's exactly knocking your door down giving you commissions, is it?" asked Jonesy as he skillfully turned their supper, a meagre-looking chicken, on a spit above the flames. "Me advice to you is just to let it go."

"I am not letting it go," declared Ishiro stubbornly. "I'm your elder, Little Jane. I give the commands, you listen."

"Well, that's exactly what I've been sayin'," answered Little Jane cheekily. "I'm too young to give commands and have 'em listened to, even if I can shout like a captain.

Ain't likely those seamen at the bar'll take me as their lord and master. That's just plain facts, Ishiro. Among the two of us what knows navigation, it's got to be you who captains the ship."

"No, no. I can't." Ishiro sighed. "You're too young to remember …" He rubbed a wrinkled hand over his tired face. "Look, long as you sees you're in the wrong —"

"But I ain't. It were wrong to volunteer you without your say-so, I allow. But I were right in wanting you for captain."

Villienne, who was busy drawing diagrams of barnacles in his notebook, looked up with interest. "What's that now? Ishiro for captain? Who'll be the cook then?"

"Jonesy cooks," suggested Little Jane. "We don't need Ishiro for that."

"Hmmm, interesting theory," replied the magistrate with a glance at the barkeep's unsanitary dinner preparations, "but just because Jonesy can roast a bit of meat on a spit, doesn't mean Mr. Ishiro here can captain a ship. What experience does he have?"

The rest of the party fell silent. Villienne was the only one present who did not know of the disaster fifteen years before. The memory of it stung so much that Ishiro, the formerly stalwart captain of the sunken *Newton*, had refused any position aboard ship of greater responsibility than cook since.

The fear of another such tragedy rested uneasily at the bottom of everyone's mind. Ever since the incident, no joy on Smuggler's Bay could ever be complete. That past horror was always there, dirtying the margin of the

story of their lives. It gnawed at the hem of every pleasure and smudged the clarity of every bright venture. Even
Little Jane, who had been born after the tragedy, felt the
subtle influence of the incident on her life. It was due to
the destruction of the *Golden Fleece* and the *Newton* that
there were no other children around Little Jane's age on
Smuggler's Bay. With most of the island's men lost in the
disaster, it had taken time for the many widows to begin
again. Still others had left the island after, never to return.

Now, as Ishiro stomped off to deal with a last-minute
supply of rope, Jonesy listened to Little Jane tell the story
of the ill-fated *Newton* to Villienne. Of all the people
who'd tried to talk Ishiro into resuming command over
the years, Jonesy realized, Little Jane might actually have
a chance of succeeding where others had always failed.
After all, Ishiro couldn't very well throw a bottle of *sake* at
Little Jane the way he had at Jonesy the last time the barkeep accidentally mentioned the *Newton*, now could he?
Unlikely, mused Jonesy wryly. After all, he'd been forced
to sell every last bottle at the market.

Villienne listened intently to Little Jane's tale of the
Golden Fleece and the *Newton*. When Little Jane came to
the end, the magistrate had to dry his eyes and blow his
nose before he could comment in any magisterial capac-
ity. By this time, Ishiro had returned from his errand and
stood, arms crossed defiantly, in the doorway.

"Be that as it may, I still feel our Little Jane is correct in
electing you captain, if only for purely financial reasons,"
Villienne finally said, looking up at the cook. "Between hir-
ing the crew and purchasing our supplies, we've completely

depleted our coffers. The only captain we can afford is one who'll work for free. That makes you and Little Jane the only ones with any proper knowledge of navigation."

"But I'm fifteen years out of practice," protested Ishiro.

"No, you're not," insisted Little Jane. "I seen you with me parents, going over the naval charts, advising them in their quarters below decks. You know how to navigate and manage men. I'll help you, I promise. Please, Ishiro." She finished with a pleading look that would have put a baby harp seal to shame.

Ishiro opened his mouth to protest, but found he was unable to say no to those enormous eyes.

"All right," he said. "I'll do it."

"To Captain Ishiro!" said Little Jane, toasting an imaginary glass.

"Hurrah!" shouted Villienne, lifting a specimen jar back at her.

Little Jane grinned, then ran over and gave an uncomfortable looking Ishiro a big hug.

"Thank you," she whispered in his ear as she embraced him. "You'll see. We'll be the best crew you ever had. You won't regret it for a minute, I swear."

Chapter Four

The Nameless Isle

Ned Ronk scowled as the rest of the crew of the *Panacea* trooped out on deck to see the captain disembark for the Nameless Isle with his chosen landing party.

Ned thought everyone on the *Panacea* would treat him like a hero after the capture of the *Pieces of Eight*. After all, it was only with his help that the ship had been secured, wasn't it? And what thanks did he get? Instead of being celebrated, he was treated like a pariah. Oh, he was rewarded handsomely for his service, to be sure. Yet the coin he had been given was precious little use to Ned while they remained at sea, which they seemed most likely to do until that loony Madsea found his treasure.

It had been a long time since Ned had served on a Crown ship. He'd forgotten the disdain they held you in if you weren't an officer or a gentleman. There had been no officers on the *Pieces of Eight* — and certainly no gentlemen — and the captains had been so loose about rank that they'd even supped with their crew. Now he had to take orders from that little snot of a midshipman, Jesper. Though he'd always sailed before the mast, Ned was dismayed to find himself still only granted a mere able seaman's status on the *Panacea*, after all he'd done.

Unfortunately, the *Panacea* already had herself a bosun, a huge Cornish man named Kingly. Ned Ronk had challenged Kingly in the mess hall for his job, only to belatedly discover the man's successful side career as a bare-knuckle boxer.

Then there was the confusion surrounding the pirate captains' "son" — really Rufus, the cabin boy from the *Pieces of Eight*, who Madsea's men had mistaken for Bonnie Mary and Long John's child. Of course, Ned was the one to alert the captain to the unfortunate case of mistaken identity. But were the officers grateful? Oh no. They actually *blamed* him.

Ned eyed one of the large orange birds flapping overhead. They still gave him the creeps, those things. Surprise, surprise, not one of the *Panacea*'s sailors had thought to delay the consumption of massive quantities of orange bird meat until they could monitor the effects of the obnoxious orange fowl on the human digestive tract. *If the whole lot of them get thoroughly sick with the runs as a result, it will serve them right,* he thought.

Despite his lack of status on board, Ned still found some consolation in the pitiable state of his former captains.

How delightful it was to see Silver, the man who'd flogged him so mercilessly aboard the *Pieces*, thrust up on deck in chains. Ned savoured the sight of his former captain leaning on a pair of uneven crutches. Chains hung from his wrists, tangling themselves up in his sticks, hobbling him still further. All his dandyish clothes had been replaced with dirty sailor's slops and his half-empty pant leg flapped behind him like a tattered old flag in the wind.

Pleased by the sight, Ned turned his attention to Bonnie Mary. She looked small and filthy, more of a dockside jade than a respectable captain, with her matted braids tied up in a bit of torn rag, tattered split-skirt indecently revealing her bare brown ankles to all. Against his will, he recalled what he had once felt for Bonnie Mary and still could not help a few wishful old fantasies from clouding his senses. He remembered a jest he'd made, back long ago, when they were all still friends, and how her whole face seemed to smile when anything amused her. He thought of her happy green eye, deep as the heart of an emerald sea, framed by lashes dark as ink.

Ned forced himself back to reality, a place where Bonnie Mary turned her good side away and his skin still stung from the lashes she'd snapped across his back.

He noticed her blind blue eye weeping now — as well it should for what she'd done, he thought. It had always rather irritated him before, how she'd often dab at it with one of those loud, colourful handkerchiefs that she kept. He'd always considered it one of her silly affectations, much like Silver's predilection for ridiculous feathered hats. Now he watched with cold detachment as she tried to wipe it off on her shirt sleeve.

Even from where he stood in the ship's bow, he could hear her loud, bossy voice.

"Where's me daughter?" she demanded. "Ain't any of you found Little Jane yet?"

"Shut up," ordered the guard, striking her. Long John struggled with his crutches as he tried to grab at the guard, but his own minder only yanked him back, nearly causing him to topple over in the process.

Bonnie Mary seemed to quiet herself, her gaze returning to the approaching shadow of the island's massive volcanic cone. Resolutely, she turned away to the port side, her eyes finding Ned Ronk's. She met his sinister stare coldly, her head held high.

Ned Ronk's expression of contempt died quickly on his features, and he felt a sudden chill. It seemed impossible, yet he was certain her dead eye actually *looked* at him now; looked and saw something it abhorred with all its blighted sight. In the shadow of the Nameless Isle it burned pure blue as a gas flame with her hatred, a feeling untempered by anything so prosaic as the rule of law, keen only to devour and destroy.

A wave of panic crashed over him. Just as quickly though, he came to his senses, remembering with sudden relief the fatal plans Madsea had in store for the two pirates. The captains would be sent to England to be hanged once Madsea had his treasure, he had been told. Either that or they'd die on the island. Either way, he had nothing to fear, not really.

Ned glanced to his captain for comfort. Madsea was on the deck in uniform for the first time in weeks, barking out orders for Lieutenant Jesper to relate to the crew. For such a narrow-chested man, the captain cut a surprisingly strong figure.

Only Doc Lewiston noticed how the sweat glistened on Madsea's feverish brow. The doctor looked over at his two other patients, wishing he could do something about their chains.

"Here, m'dear," he said gently, handing Bonnie Mary his own clean handkerchief to wipe her weeping eye.

"Much obliged," she whispered humbly.

Doc Lewiston also noted, with some discomfort, that the guard assigned to Silver, a certain Able-Seaman Snepper, seemed to derive a tad too much pleasure from the exercise of yanking the pirate about by his chains, as if he was trying to make him fall. So far, the pirate had remained upright, though just barely.

It upset Doc Lewiston's sensibilities to see such pointless cruelty. How had he ever managed to involve himself in something so completely repulsive to his senses, both moral and medical?

Oblivious to the speculations of his crew, Captain Madsea walked the well-scrubbed boards of the *Panacea* with feverish intensity. His ever-present riding crop swished at his side like a panther's tail, alighting on the back of any sailor he perceived to be slacking in his duties. Today no detail, no matter how small, escaped the lamp-like scrutiny of his gaze. After all, today was the day he would have his revenge. Today success was guaranteed.

The ship that Villienne commandeered had originally been the *Duke of York*, but as it had only been painted with the word *York* before they took possession, it quickly became known as the *Yorkman* to the crew. This pleased Captain Ishiro. Although he knew ships were usually given female names, he couldn't help feeling there was something essentially male about the modern, muscular lines of the *Yorkman*.

It had only taken Ishiro a day to assemble the crew and bring all the supplies on board. During this time, Villienne kept him well supplied with green lichen drinks, which, although they tasted disgusting, seemed to genuinely improve his health. Surprisingly, he was feeling even stronger today. No ghost of his old comrades could begrudge him this, he thought. After all, sad as it was, those men were long dead. The crew of the *Pieces* was, in all probability, still very much alive and in desperate need of rescue. It felt strange to reacquaint himself with his old ways of command after so many years, skills he'd never expected to rely on again. Still, at that moment, it truly felt as if no intervening years had passed.

It was Little Jane's job to make sure the ship did not leave without Villienne, who despite having crammed his room on board full to bursting with strange vials, inks, and huge sheaves of paper, was in a constant state of running back out to purchase more "absolutely essential items" in town.

When the ship finally did set sail, Villienne took to sea travel easily, displaying none of the seasickness landlubbers often did on the choppy seas. Unfortunately, the same could not be said of Jonesy. Only now did Little Jane begin to appreciate the great sacrifice the barkeep had made by coming on their journey. Jonesy was deathly afraid of water and prone to the worst bouts of seasickness she'd ever seen. And while many of the crew laughed at the fearsome-looking bartender humbled by even the gentlest rocking of the waves, Villienne did not. After all, if anyone could sympathize with a man out of his element, it was the magistrate of Smuggler's Bay.

Villienne took it upon himself to hold the bartender by the shoulders whenever Jonesy began to look the least bit off-colour and steer him directly to the nearest railing or scupper for a quiet vomit. Then, while Jonesy remained a captive audience, Villienne would distract him with a poem or two.

As ridiculous as Little Jane first thought it, she soon observed that Villienne's poetry recitations really did seem to do the trick in focusing Jonesy's energies on something other than the rocking of the boat. For his part, Villienne, always starved for an appreciative audience, seemed pleased by his new association.

The biggest problem with Jonesy's seasickness was that it left him unable to properly tend to his cooking duties. Little Jane soon found herself thrust from cook's mate into the position of cook herself. This did not bother her much, as most of her job involved stirring a big pot that Jonesy would come by and add things to when he was not otherwise occupied with hurling the contents of his stomach overboard, but it was dreadfully dull. Little Jane soon ended up borrowing some of Villienne's "absolutely essential" books just to relive the tedium.

She'd come upon the open crate of books in Villienne's stateroom while the magistrate was otherwise occupied above decks. Little Jane's attention was instantly riveted by the uppermost book in the stack, a green-clad volume with the title, *Robin Hood*, printed in faded gilt letters on the cover. This book was like no other Little Jane had ever seen. For one, it was her favourite colour. Second, it mentioned something that sounded awfully like "robbery" right in the title. On these two facts alone, Little Jane knew she'd have to investigate further.

She cracked the book's cover as she mechanically stirred her pot with its long wooden ladle down in the galley kitchen. She was instantly riveted, borne far away from her own troubles, into a land of knights and forester-outlaws. When she did not understand something she read, she looked to the pictures of people brandishing bows and arrows for explanation and soon found she understood far more than she did not.

Little Jane was no stranger to books, not exactly, but what books her parents owned were straightforward compilations of coordinates, star charts, and other reference guides practical for sailing life. Books were expensive and few people aboard could read with ease. As a result, all the soul-searing stories of grand adventure Little Jane loved were told aloud over the glow of the Spyglass's fire, rather than found between cardboard covers.

Of course, she had seen similar books in the dusty, unappealing windows of shops in America that closed their doors to people like her. In England they were held in the laps of dour black-clad men in high collars and women in puffy dresses. But nothing in the setting she found them in, or the type of people she'd seen reading them, seemed relevant to her. In her life of constant travel she'd seen some truly odd things that people in different places did for fun and had tried plenty of them. Yet here was a ridiculously entertaining pastime, hidden in plain sight from her nearly all her life!

To discover just the sort of stories she loved, to be had and enjoyed whenever she wished, was nothing short of a revelation. No longer would she be forced to wait until the end of the day, when her father was freed up from work to hear a tale, or rely solely on her own fancy for entertainment. She could borrow books from Villienne, or even pick up her own from some of the ports they stopped at. Where no inkling of such potential had ever existed before, new possibilities sprang up in her mind. Although she was under too much pressure to reflect on it then, in later years, Little Jane would look back upon the discovery of Villienne's books as one of the events that nudged her toward a different path than the one she'd always assumed she would travel. But that day she only read seeking escape, a passage through that trap door in the attic of her mind, to places she'd never dreamed of before.

The *Yorkman* had been rolling and tossing all morning on the rough sea, but as it hit a particularly large swell, the ship suddenly lurched to one side, sending cups and plates crashing to the floor of the galley and spilling a large pot of gravy over the pages of the book. Cursing, Little

Jane jumped up, flannel in hand, to clean up the mess. Then, just as she was dabbing gravy off a picture of the Sheriff of Nottingham, Villienne poked his head in to see if she was all right.

"I'm sorry," she confessed. "I had no business rooting around in your things. I weren't stealing, honest. I was just curious, that's all. I would've returned it as soon as I finished."

Villienne took the book from Little Jane and studied it gravely. "My professional opinion as an almost-doctor is that the Sheriff of Nottingham should survive his gravy accident, to clash with Robin Hood another day. But say, what did you think of the story?"

"Th-the story? I didn't finish it," she admitted, pleased he wasn't angry.

"See that you read the rest then, before returning it to me," he said, handing the book back with a smile.

"Thank you." Little Jane beamed up at him. Then she had a sudden flash of inspiration. "May I ask you something?" she ventured.

"Of course," Villienne answered. "What is it?"

"You seem to know a great deal about words. Tell me, what d'ye think these mean?" Little Jane unwound the fabric from Melvin, her mother's wooden sword, so she could show the magistrate the mysterious words carved into the hilt.

"Masthead, East, Lamp, Vergaloo, in Nakika," Villienne read, rolling each word slowly around his mouth, as if tasting it for meaning. "That's an odd set if I ever did hear one. I must say, it seems like gibberish to me," he admitted. "May I ask what you call your sword?"

"Melvin," she replied bashfully. "A silly name I know. A sword's supposed t'be named for a woman."

"I always thought if I ever chose to name my blade, I'd call it Eurydice," mused Villienne. "Or perhaps Eunice. Always liked the name Eunice. Of course I have no blade, so that is rather beside the point. Melvin *is* quite a strange name for a sword, though, no doubt about it. How ever did you come to choose it?"

"I didn't," she said. "Me mum just told me that was the name. I guess it were her what named him and carved in the words."

"That seems possible." He stood for a moment, stroking his chin, deep in thought. "Wait a tick! It isn't a strange name at all. And it's not gibberish either."

Villienne pulled a small book of poetry from his breast pocket and opened it up. "Look here. It's a type of poem."

"Poem?"

"An acrostic," explained Villienne. "The first letter in each line, when read downward, spells out a word. Now look," he remarked excitedly, "Masthead East Lamp Vergaloo in Nakika. Take all the first letters of those words and what do they spell?"

"Melvin!" exclaimed Little Jane. "The name of the sword. If I know me mum, it's probably some type of code." She smacked her fist on her thigh in frustration. "If only we knew what it meant!"

"Maybe I can help you there," said Villienne. "A masthead is a …"

"I know what a masthead is. I'm a sailor. It's the top crossed part o' the mast," said Little Jane impatiently. "And east is east. And a lamp is a lamp, I suppose. But what about vergaloo? What in blazes is a vergaloo anyway?"

"Oh, that's easy," replied Villienne.

"It *is*?" asked Little Jane, raising one eyebrow. "'Cause nobody else around here seems to know."

"A virga*leau*, as it is properly pronounced in French, is an ornamental pear tree," explained Villienne.

"An ornamental pear tree? Blow me down!" Little Jane laughed. "Don't tell me you know what that's got to do with anything?"

"I haven't a clue. All I know is that my Aunt Cornelia used to have one in her garden."

"And Nakika? You figure that one out, too?"

"I think it's fairly obvious. Na Kika is the octopus god of the South Pacific Samoan islanders."

"Unbelievable," said Little Jane excitedly. "Villienne, you're a genius."

"I just read a good deal more than is good for me," he replied with charming modesty.

"I wish I knew all you did," Little Jane said wistfully. "Things'd be well easy then."

"You have no idea." Villienne sighed as he stared down ruefully at his hands. As usual they were covered in ink stains from his leaky fountain pen and odd little burn marks, the result of numerous chemistry accidents. Not the hands of a workingman, nor a gentleman either. "So much folly," he confided to her. "Whatever knowledge I possess, I lack even the most rudimentary grasp of how to make money. If only I could invent a chemical agent to remove lime-scale or hard-to-treat-stains, I wouldn't be so hopeless. A well-spoken repository of fundamentally useless knowledge is all I am."

"Why, you have lots of knowledge that's worth knowing," said Little Jane. "Just be a matter of waiting for the proper occasion of using it is all."

"One could wait a lifetime for such an occasion when it comes to my talents," he remarked wryly.

"Maybe. But whenever I gets a piece of knowledge I ain't able to make use of right away, I writes it down so I don't forget it. I used to have a little book for it, too. I wrote down all the things I'd be needing to know about how to be a good pirate."

"What was the book called?"

"How to Be a Good Pirate."

"Oh."

"Only thing is, I can't find it. Must've gone down with the *Pieces of Eight*, I reckon."

"Ah," said Villienne, thinking hard about the title of Little Jane's book. Something about it seemed vaguely cockeyed to him. He was troubled by the concept that a seemingly intelligent girl's greatest desire in the world was to become "a good pirate," whatever that meant.

"Aren't the words *good* and *pirate* mutually exclusive?" Villienne mused. "Isn't it common knowledge that being a sea-faring outlaw with a price on one's head and questionable dietary standards, pleasant as your parents may be, is still a destiny best to be avoided, not pursued?"

"I suppose next ye'll try to convince me I ought to stay home and tend the inn," she snorted. "Be happy as a wife or spinster or some other such proper womanly

70

profession, like them skirts back in England."

"You misunderstand me, Jane. Obviously, you love the sea, but there are other ways to indulge in that ardour without snatching others' belongings and being so free and easy with the law. "

"Like what?" she asked suspiciously.

"There are ways," he insisted, "if one only has the courage to try something different. I've lived in London and seen marvellous things done by people both high and low, and a great number of them women, too. Why, I once met a woman who translated the entire English language into a sequence of ones and zeroes, and a man who could animate disembodied frogs' legs simply by passing electrical current through them!"

"That's great n'all, but what use would animated frogs' legs or that ones and zeroes talk be to us aboard ship? Wouldn't help no one change course in a storm or swab the deck. And a pirate's life ain't as free and easy as you be thinking either."

"I hardly think the life appears easy," said Villienne. "Just look at your parents and all they've been through."

"I wish I *could* look at them, instead of listening to you," retorted Little Jane rudely, blinking back tears. "Ain't your business telling me the way they live is wrong, when that's all they ever knowed and them not here to defend their selves from slander!"

Villienne placed a hand gently on her shoulder. "Come now. I meant no offence by it. We'll see them safe to rights. We've a strong wind at our backs and we'll catch up, you'll see."

"Aye, maybe," mumbled Little Jane as Villienne retired to the companionway. She had too much to think about; between the words on Melvin, books dipped in gravy, and languages made of numbers, her head was spinning. Meanwhile, there was the Nameless Isle to prepare for, and finding her parents to worry about.

Now was no time to dwell on such things, she chided herself before returning resolutely to stirring the soup, pausing only to read the last chapter of *Robin Hood* to see how the story ended.

Chapter Five

More Trouble Than They're Worth

Little Jane was not the only member of the Silver family thinking hard that day. As the launch party assembled, Bonnie Mary busied herself contemplating all the parts of their plan that might not work.

It galled her that Jim looked so carefree and cheery, so childishly pleased to be unchained at last, crutches be damned. His delight at being outside and upright showed so clearly on his broad, expressive face that it nearly broke her heart.

Bonnie Mary could read him like a book. No, she amended, easier than that; unlike books, Jim's weathered countenance held no secrets from her. She knew that at that moment he was thoroughly occupied with the feeling of the wind ruffling his hair, the smell of the briny air curling in his nostrils, and the glare of the sun as it glinted off the rolling waves.

She, too, was relieved to be able to turn around without meeting a wall in every direction; however, she could not lose herself in the sensations of the sea as he could. Not today, at any rate. It was her curse to keep on thinking. Thinking about how much closer they were to the impossible task before them — and the distinct possibility that they would die trying to accomplish it.

"Courage, me love," whispered Long John, suddenly appearing beside her. Gently, he stroked her arm with his hand, but all she felt was the desire to brush it away. Subtle shifts in her posture gave away her increasing edginess, like a change in the atmosphere, or static in the air before a rainstorm.

"Courage? That's just a fancy word for there ain't no more options," she muttered.

The launch was lowered down to the water, hitting the water with a soft splash. The sails unfurled and luffed in the strong breeze as the party set out.

Twelve people set sail aboard the launch toward the Nameless Isle that day. Captain Madsea, Doc Lewiston, and Darsa, Madsea's steward, were the only ones she and Long John recognized by sight. Their numbers were filled out by other seamen, including Kingly, the bosun, and six others chosen by Madsea to work the sails and rudder. Would twelve make it back, as well? Bonnie Mary had no illusions on that score. Jesper, the ship's lieutenant, was left in command of the *Panacea*, with Savignon, the quartermaster, to help him with the crew and captives until their captain's return — assuming he did return, that is.

The ex-crew of the *Pieces of Eight* stared anxiously after their former captains as the launch made its way slowly toward the island. Madsea, especially, was the target of a substantial number of dark looks from men who prided themselves on their ability to hold grudges for as long as it took to get satisfaction.

Lieutenant Jesper rocked back uneasily on his heels. He hoped the captain didn't do anything stupid to the two pirate captains while they were on the island. *The last thing this sodding tub needs is a prisoners' revolt*, he thought grimly.

As the launch bobbed along, Bonnie Mary reassured herself by going over the strategy she'd hashed out with Long John days ago in the brig. The way she figured it, they had five major weapons on their side in their war against Fetz on the island.

First was the knife, still secreted away in her corset. It would be hers for the quick, deft stab in the ribs to an enemy standing close. Second were Jim's crutches, ideal instruments for cracking open a man's head like a coconut in his strong, capable hands. Third and fourth were weapons of a geographical nature. The two pirate captains were the only ones who knew both the location of the treasure cave *and* the secret way to get there.

Stalling for time was the best strategy, they both agreed. Bonnie Mary hoped Madsea wouldn't discover they were taking him on a roundabout route until it was too late. Taking the long way around meant they could waste plenty of time climbing the island's jagged rocks and crossing the moat at the widest point before Madsea got wise to what they were doing. The longer it took to get to their destination, the more likely the party from the *Panacea* was to run afoul of weapon number five, the wildlife of the island, a danger Bonnie Mary prayed she and Jim might avoid.

She hoped enough of Madsea's men would be incapacitated by the time they made it to the treasure cave that she and Jim would have a fighting chance of defeating whoever was left. A long shot, of course, but it was the only scheme they came up with that offered any possibility of success.

If they managed to get to the cave, circumstances might prove more favourable. Along with the coins, gold, and jewels accumulated in its inner recesses there were also a few weapons they'd left on the island, deeming them too rich or impractical for everyday use, or too small to join the impressive display behind the bar at the Spyglass.

Among the weapons she distinctly remembered storing were a pair of tiny one-shot Italian pistols, a ruby studded ceremonial Punjabi dagger, and an ivory-handled machete intended for splitting coconuts. Not exactly a proper ship's arsenal, but useful nonetheless.

If they managed to kill Madsea, she and Jim could hole up in the cave for at least a few days. They could even eat the peculiar orange birds in a pinch. There were always birds in the cave when they visited, so she assumed there were nests nearby. Drinking water could come from the condensation in the cave or captured rainfall. It would be hard, but Bonnie Mary was determined that Fetz would never win. If they held out long enough, she reasoned, the rest of his party might just give up and leave. It was their leader, despite his frail state, who kept them moving, animated by his spirit and purpose. She hoped the rest only cared about getting their pay.

"We can wear them out," Jim had promised her with a confident smile. "Just look at Fetz. His strength is flagging already."

Yet, as the jagged rocks rose up to greet them, Long John looked more like the one whose strength was flagging. He sagged against the gunwales, his eyes on the cliffs looming above them, growing closer with every gust of wind in the small boat's sails. And Bonnie Mary, who knew her Jim better than anyone else alive, knew he was only just beginning to realize the true enormity of the task ahead.

Back on the *Panacea*, Ned Ronk's mind was still consumed with the idea of the treasure on the island.

It is a truth universally acknowledged that, standing astride a powerful sea-going vessel, with little to do, one's thoughts automatically turn to treasure — how to obtain it, how to keep it, and how to steal it away from everyone else.

Following this common train of thought, it occurred to Ned Ronk that one of the great benefits of serving aboard the *Pieces of Eight* was that, like most pirate captains, Silver and Bright divided the loot equally among captains and crew, never taking a greater share.

Sourly, he doubted that would be the case aboard the *Panacea*. The thought of all that treasure going to that loony Madsea galled him rotten. Surely, he, Ned

Ronk, should get a bigger piece of the pie. After all, he was the one who sabotaged the *Pieces of Eight*'s fighting capabilities and delivered the pirate captains into Madsea's hands. Surely he deserved to be rewarded with more than the piddling fee he'd received from the doctor back in Havana.

He frowned. What a man *deserved* had little to do with what he received on this earth, of that Ned Ronk was certain: The only way to get what was owed to you was to take it yourself. This time he would get his fair share, he thought determinedly, no matter what he needed to do to get it.

Despite his lack of conventional sea knowledge, Villienne was correct in his prediction of good winds for the rest of the *Yorkman*'s voyage. The weather was as perfect as it could ever be at sea, and with the *Yorkman* in possession of the most up-to-date ship's features, they cut through the ocean like a knife through butter. (In fact, unbeknownst to the crew, the *Yorkman* was well on its way to making the Nameless Isle in nearly half the time it took the older, less daringly built *Panacea*.)

Ishiro watched Little Jane jump restlessly from ratline to ratline before landing on the deck. The wind tinkled the golden key of Melvin's case that she now wore in her ear as she looked through the spyglass at the expanse of blue that lay ahead.

"I saw it," she announced excitedly, pointing. "The island, it's not too far — a half-day's journey, maybe less.

We could make it by morning if we sail on hard through the night."

"All right," said Ishiro. "I'll give the command. You sure you still want to go with us when we make the island?"

"Aye, Captain. There's no way I'd stay on the *Yorkman* while you go rescue me own parents," she answered firmly.

Many a member of the *Yorkman*'s crew crossed himself as the first flock of orange birds lit on the mizzenmast early the next morning. They were still quite a distance from the island, but the lazy birds could ride quite a way on air currents alone.

Ishiro, of course, was well aware of the birds' reputation as bowl-bashing cuisine. Before leaving Jamaica he'd taken the precaution of packing the ship's larder with the best salted beef and jerk chicken the island had to offer, and plenty of coconuts to season them with. Hopefully this would prevent the men from entertaining any notion of eating the peculiar orange fowl. Vigilance was crucial. It only took the consumption of one bird to leave a man incapacitated for a week, Ishiro knew, which is why it sometime helps to have a captain who's also been a cook.

What were the chances that Madsea was still on the island or that this was even their intended destination? Ishiro was still worried, but in his heart he believed they were nearby. At the thought of the potential confrontation, he experienced a feeling long dormant in his soul. Like an old gun dog, he twitched with anticipation for the chase. He sensed the other men were feeling the same. None were completely immune to the energy of the hunt, that momentary thirst for a little blood, a little action.

It wouldn't be long now.

Chapter Six

The Cursed Climb

The party on Madsea's launch was unhappy. They were sweaty, they were tired. And only Captain Madsea and the doctor had had the presence of mind to bring spiked climbing shoes to tackle the jagged, slippery rocks.

Now, your average rock is either jagged or slippery, but rarely both. However, the rocks that ring the Nameless Isle are covered with peculiar orange bird guano, which everyone knows is one of the slipperiest of slippery substances on earth. Vast quantities of slimy green lichen did nothing to help matters either. Here in the predator-free micro-climate of the Nameless Isle, the lichen flourished in much greater profusion than it ever did in Smuggler's Bay. Here it never had a chance to dry out, thanks to the spray of sea water crashing into the rocks with predictable frequency, 365 days of the year. Here, thin leather sandals and flimsy deck slippers provided little to no purchase, eventually forcing the *Panacea*'s resentful crew to tackle the island with bare hands and feet.

Or foot, if you happened to have just one. For Long John, the scramble over the guano-stained, wet lichen covered rocks was a terrible trial, worse than he'd anticipated due to his still-healing injuries, the stifling heat, and a certain spotty-faced seaman named Snepper who'd been entrusted with the task of forcing him to keep up with the rest of the group. Mostly, this involved the seaman jabbing the pirate in the rear with the stock of his rifle whenever Long John's pace slackened (or whenever Long John's pace was just fine, but Seaman Snepper felt the urge to jab him anyway). After an hour of exertion, Long John decided to forego the further abuse of his buttocks and sit. He eased himself down on a rocky ledge to take a much-needed rest, stripping off his shirt to expose his back to a blessed hint of a breeze.

He took a sip of lukewarm water from his canteen. "Say there," he began, trying to engage Snepper in conversation. "I ever tell you about the time me and the missus went hiking in the Andes?"

"No," snapped Snepper, picking up his rifle.

Jab. Jab.

"Get moving."

Long John balanced listlessly, resigned to obey out of sheer exhaustion. To argue would take more effort than he could muster at the moment. He could see the rest of the party through the wedge-shaped gap between the rocks below. They were farther ahead, picking their careful way through the jagged fangs of rock.

They travelled silently on, at one point forced to walk where the water came up to their ankles, the stone they stood on submerged beneath their feet. The ocean surged and foamed threateningly around them, misting their bodies with a fine cooling spray. Later, they found themselves high up on the stones, forced to jump between small gaps in the rocks. Long John could always make out Bonnie Mary, even at a distance. She was at the front of the party, and the only one still wearing a shirt. All the men had long since stripped down to breeches like him, their bare backs shining in the pitiless glare of the sun.

"Keep moving," growled Snepper.

Jab. Jab.

Long John wished in vain for the crutches he'd had on the ship. They would have been perfect to crack over the infuriating Snepper's skull. Now, that would stop the infernal jabbing. Much to his annoyance, though, he could still see the sturdy wood implements bobbing mockingly along up ahead in the distance, where they were strapped to the steward's back.

"What're you looking at?" sneered Snepper. "Keep moving."

Jab, jab

"Hope that thing goes off in yer face one day, mate," Long John snarled at him. Steeling himself for another jump, he flicked his braided queue over his shoulder. The sweaty tail of hair stuck to his back like a leech. Then he braced his foot between two rocks and launched himself forward, reaching out for the next punishing hand hold.

Long John wasn't the only one feeling out of sorts on the trek. In the bleary haze of the midday sun, Bonnie Mary was starting to have some serious misgivings. Her thoughts moved sluggishly as she struggled to remember every detail of the plan. *So blasted hot.* It felt like her brain was baking. It would be *so* tempting, with the secret path just a mile away from where they now stood, to pack the whole "long way around" idea in and just take the easy route.

Don't think about it, she told herself. *Wear them fellows out. Give rescuers time to reach us.* Assuming any rescuers were coming, that is. She tossed her head to get a few stray braids out of her eyes, only to have the wind whip them right back in place again. Damp tendrils of hair stuck to her temples and a stripe of sweat ran down her spine, plastering her shirt to her back.

Bonnie Mary willed herself to keep moving, climbing over peaks and leaping deep crevices frothing with ocean water; from rock to rock like a Billy goat, with the rest of the group straggling along in single file behind her. Every few minutes she'd look over her shoulder toward the back of the pack, checking to make sure Jim was still there. He was, although she could see he was flagging, now more than ever.

At last she made it to a rocky outcropping with a flat, wide ledge. It was the first moderately level surface Bonnie Mary had been on in what seemed like hours. A high, craggy rock beside the ledge even created a pleasant bit of shade. There was a round depression in the flat floor that formed a bowl where a pool of water had collected. The shade of the high rock kept the water miraculously cool in the heat of the day. She dipped a finger in and tasted it: freshwater, not salt.

Bonnie Mary cupped her hands and drank deeply. She noticed a healthy patch of lush green lichen growing around the ridge of the rocky bowl and using her fingernails she managed to scrape a large strip of it off. She tore it in half, popped one part in her mouth, and quickly pocketed the rest before the remainder of the company caught up.

Fetzcaro Madsea leapt across the gulf between the rocks, staggering a little as he landed on the ledge beside her. "What the hell're you doing?"

"Sitting," she replied, swallowing her piece of the lichen in a single gulp. Calmly, she studied his face. There were two bright red spots on his cheeks and he seemed to be having trouble focusing his eyes.

"Well, stop it. You have to get up … we have to … we have to make … to make …" Madsea's voice trailed off. He coughed, staggered once more, then collapsed to his knees and tipped forward, his head landing in a shocked Bonnie Mary's lap.

Doc Lewiston landed with a thump on the ledge just in time to see his captain collapse.

"Quick! Someone fetch me water," cried the doctor.

Without thinking, Bonnie Mary scooped up some of the water from the depression on the ledge with her canteen and handed it to the doctor.

Doc Lewiston poured a little water in the captain's mouth. He dampened the tail of his shirt and dabbed it over the captain's overheated face. Madsea spluttered and choked, but quickly revived under these ministrations. It was clear that the captain's energy level was at a serious low, so Doc Lewiston pronounced it as good a time as any for a bit of rest and victuals.

"Ahoy there," panted Long John. "Looks as if they've stopped up ahead. Wonder what the trouble is."

His captor said nothing. He was too busy expelling his breakfast over the side of a rock. The orange bird cuisine was doing its work at last, thought Long John with pleasure. He left the miserable seaman to this unpleasant activity and forged on toward Bonnie Mary and the rest of the party.

Bonnie Mary, Doc Lewiston, the bosun Kingly, and a weakened Madsea formed an awkward tableau on the rock. The other sailors sat crowded together on a rocky shelf nearby. Chipp, one of the cook's mates from the *Panacea*, took the opportunity to hand out parcels of salted orange bird meat to the famished troops.

Doc Lewiston tried to coax Madsea into eating his meat ration, but the captain refused. The doctor noticed Kingly wasn't eating either, which was strange because the bosun could usually be relied upon to devour anything on his plate, even maggoty old ship's biscuit. The stout bosun's face was unnaturally pale as he held his distended belly. Yes, it was decidedly odd, thought the doctor, but he had no time to look after the man. Something had to be done about the captain … and soon.

"He don't look so good, and we ain't a quarter through the journey yet. I'd be concerned if I was you, Doctor," said Bonnie Mary. "Maybe we oughtta head back to the ship."

"Please, let me think," pleaded Doc Lewiston, dabbing his own overheated brow. "I saw you drinking that water. Is it fresh?"

"I think so," replied Bonnie Mary hesitantly.

"Good enough."

Lewiston scooped some of the water from the depression into his own cup. As he dipped his tin cup in, he scraped off some of green lichen with its metal rim. The bits of lichen floated up to the surface of the water like a strange species of tea leaf.

"I once knew a doctor who'd sailed with his majesty's fleet in India," Lewiston explained. "He found patients with dehydration often improved more speedily when re-hydrated with water from multiple sources." Doc Lewiston glanced dubiously at the captain's canteen of tepid rain barrel water that they'd collected over the past week on board the *Panacea*. He poured it out and replaced it with the fresh water from his cup and handed it back to Madsea. The captain drained the canteen and handed it back.

With a sigh, Doc Lewiston dipped the cup in again, scraping off a little more lichen in the process, and refilled the canteen. He then drank the rest himself.

That might complicate things, thought Bonnie Mary, chewing meditatively on a piece of orange bird wing. She hadn't expected Madsea to drink the water from the pool. In addition, now Doc Lewiston was drinking it too. What if that little bit of lichen in it protected them from the effect of the orange bird meat? She had to talk to Jim. She stared out worriedly across the rocks, searching for him. Had he fallen without her noticing?

"Give an old tar a hand?" said a weary voice behind her.

"Jim!" She stood and reached out to help him hop across the gulf between the two rocks. He barrelled into her and they fell to the ground in an exhausted heap.

"What happened to Seaman Snepper?" asked the doctor suspiciously.

"Feeling poorly he was. Ain't said why." Long John sat down heavily and drained his canteen in a single gulp. "Oh Lordy, that's good," he said, letting out a long sigh. But the warm water failed to completely slake his thirst. "What think you of this heat, Mary?" he asked, making certain Doc Lewiston and the captain heard him.

"Bound to get worse," Bonnie Mary answered. "Why, just look at those clouds."

Lewiston peered skeptically at the three small clouds in the sky. They certainly *looked* harmless enough.

"Oh, I know what you're thinking, Doc, they looks a'right." Long John nodded. "But best beware, them's *air hotness clouds*, they is."

"Air hotness clouds?" inquired the puzzled doctor.

"Aye," agreed Bonnie Mary. "*Cumulous numulous.* Means this heat wave'll last a week."

"Maybe more," added Long John.

"We should find someplace cool to hole up," said Bonnie Mary, "or wait it out back on the ship. Try again when the heat wave's passed."

"Certainly be healthier for the captain." Long John nodded toward Madsea.

At the mention of his name, Madsea suddenly sat bolt upright. He glared right at the two pirates, his gaze quickly becoming clear and focused. "Air hotness clouds," he thundered. "I ain't heard such bunk in all me days. There's nothing unusual about them clouds. These deceitful pirates are just pulling the wool over your eyes."

He rose to his feet with uncharacteristic vigour, brushing off Darsa's proffered arm. "Mincing laggards, the lot o' you! We've got to make the other side of these rocks by nightfall. Best we make a good start of it and leave now."

He paused to size up a rather brazen orange bird that had landed on the ledge in the midst of his tirade.

"Eh? What're you looking at?" The creature seemed to be enthralled by the soles of Madsea's climbing shoes, where the shiny new metal cleats protruded from the leather, and it tilted its head quizzically up at him.

"Stupid bird!" yelled Madsea, booting the presumptuous bird off the rock. After this exertion, he paused for one of his customary coughing fits before clambering past the stunned sailors and continuing the trek over the treacherous rocks unaided.

Oddly enough, as they continued inland, Madsea

actually seemed to gain energy, while the men who had begun the quest in the heartiest of health found themselves lagging as stomach cramps and nausea overtook them one by one.

As the sun set on the Nameless Isle, the party finally climbed over the last of the deadly black rocks and arrived, exhausted beside the expanse of water that encircled the mountain at the centre of the island like a moat. They made camp on a patch of black sand that seemed to be a popular feeding ground for large numbers of the peculiar orange birds. Doc Lewiston noticed that these specimens seemed to be much larger than any they had previously encountered. A few sailors made quick work of slaughtering several of the hapless creatures, and the two pirate captains graciously offered to help cook them on a spit over an open fire in traditional *boucanier* style. The meat emerged mouth-wateringly succulent and tender.

Though he sneered at the pirate captains' pathetic attempts to ingratiate themselves with the crew, Madsea had to admit that the birds *were* deliciously prepared. In fact, he hadn't eaten so heartily in months. Doc Lewiston congratulated him on his improved appetite.

As the launch party bedded down for the night, the Nameless Isle echoed with sounds unfamiliar to the men's ears. The air around them vibrated with the hum of palm-sized mosquitoes. The eerie cries of the peculiar orange birds, still scouring the island for their missing companions now in the process of being digested by the unlucky sailors, kept all but the soundest of sleepers awake for hours.

Finally, as the moon hid her face behind a cloud and the darkness waxed complete, the birds' cries died down at last. The only noise to be heard, if one listened very, very closely, was a soft munching sound coming from the far edge of the camp.

Long John was chewing on the bit of green lichen Bonnie Mary had saved for him, making sure to swallow every last bite.

Chapter Seven

M Is for Masthead

Early the next morning, Little Jane was the first to spot the volcanic cone of the Nameless Isle rising out of the sea from her perch in the crow's nest, the highest point aboard the ship. It appeared shadowy and insubstantial, indigo-coloured from so far away. Yet no matter how many times Little Jane saw it, the sight of that mountain never failed to elicit in her a shiver of delight. To her the Nameless Isle was not cursed. It was an enchanted place; a land scooped out of fog by giants' hands, made for herself and her family alone.

From her perch she saw the lights of the *Panacea* through the morning mist, blazing brightly even at such a distance. Apparently, the enemy captain was not expecting visitors, for nothing had been done to disguise the *Panacea*'s presence. The ship was anchored well off-shore, away from the rocky shallows near the island.

Informed of their enemy's position, Ishiro immediately changed the *Yorkman*'s course, and they approached the island from the leeward side, taking the ship the long way around instead of sailing to the point they usually anchored at. The element of surprise was important, Ishiro explained, as the *Yorkman* was a smaller ship than the *Panacea* and, although much speedier, might be more easily sunk.

They extinguished every lantern aboard in the dense fog and tied the sails taut to prevent any luffing sounds from reaching the ears of the *Panacea*'s crew. The plan was to sneak up and take the *Panacea* unawares.

They made their way carefully around the island, the *Yorkman*'s shallower hull allowing them to manoeuvre the ship closer to the rocky shore than they would have been able to in the *Pieces of Eight*.

As the *Yorkman* hugged the shore, Little Jane watched the jagged peaks of the island's rocks slide slowly past like the spikes on a vicious dog's collar. Jonesy lifted his head from the bowsprit to stare at the forbidding black crags, dotted here and there with impressive growths of green lichen. "Well," he said to Villienne with a wave of his hand, "you think your sample kit can fit it all?"

"It's a botanist's dream!" exclaimed the enraptured scientist. "Just think of all the new possibilities for nomenclature."

As Villienne ran off below decks to find his specimen kit, "just in case," Little Jane took out her spyglass.

The magistrate emerged a few minutes later with a butterfly net, a jumble of sample jars, cutting tools, and several test tubes stuffed with gauze.

"Ahoy, Captain," Little Jane suddenly called out. "Ishiro, what d'ye make o' that?"

She handed him the spyglass and pointed toward the shore, where a tall wooden pole stuck out like a toothpick from between two black fangs of rock.

"Looks like a piece of an old wreck," he said dismissively. "Ship's mast fetched up on the rocky shore. Must be years old, I'd say. Don't see mastheads crafted like *that* nowadays."

"Masthead?" Little Jane smacked her forehead with her palm. "M is for … masthead."

"Stop the ship!" All hands turned in alarm as Little Jane roared the command. Her voice reached even the highest point of the forecastle.

"What're you —"

"Ishiro, we have to drop anchor. Now!"

"Slow us down," Ishiro instructed the crew. He turned back to Little Jane. "What's going on? What's so important about that masthead?"

Little Jane waved Melvin triumphantly before him. "It's *the* masthead — the one from the code on the sword!"

"But —"

"We have to drop anchor here, get out and have a look." She turned her large eyes on Ishiro in an effort to melt his resolve.

"No," said Ishiro, a warning note in his voice.

"What?" Little Jane fell back, shaken to her core that the "big-eyes" tactic hadn't worked.

"Was it but you and me, Little Jane, I would gladly say go, but I've a whole crew here, and they be depending on me. They swore articles that, was they to come aboard, it was *not* to set foot on the Nameless Isle. I ain't going back on me promise to them."

"But Ish —"

"Little Jane, maybe you don't understand this sort of thing yet, but our best strategy is t'get to their ship and use our cannons on 'er quick as possible. Who knows? They may've already found the treasure and are fixing to leave. We've no time to waste gallivanting off after some half-baked sign on the say-so of some words carved on a sword."

Little Jane simmered visibly, but did not back down. It was time to call in reinforcements. "Jonesy, tell Ishiro we have to drop anchor."

Ishiro looked around carefully at the anxious faces of the crew. He dropped his voice a notch. "If I go with your suggestion, Little Jane, I risk mutiny from this entire crew. You don't understand, superstitions run deep 'bout this island. 'Sides, who's to say your folks ain't still on the enemy ship?"

"Because I *know* them! More still, I know me father's reputation. If you was the enemy captain and Long John Silver told *you* the coordinates where to find the treasure, would *you* trust him to give you correct directions?"

"Not bloody likely," admitted Jonesy.

"If the enemy is on that island looking for me parents' treasure, then you better believe he'll keep me mum and dad on a tight leash. Leastwise, that's what I'd do. Otherwise what's keepin' 'em from giving him the coordinates for falling straight down a lava tube, while me parents sit safe on board. Leastways, if they lead him astray and they're all on the island together, they'd be putting *themselves* in danger too and might think twice on it."

"Hmm ..." muttered Jonesy, swaying to Little Jane's side of the argument once more. "Ishiro, this business with the masthead, it stirs something in me, too." Jonesy spoke slowly as if pulling up the memory from deep within the recesses of his mind, like a fossil pulled from the depths of a tarry swamp. "Seems to me I heard tell of something akin to this before. Sometime right after Jim and Mary come back from Anguilla, I think — something about when they buried old Captain Bright on the island. I think they used it for a marker for the grave. They used the broken masthead from his ship, 'cause a masthead's shaped like cross."

Ishiro flushed at the mention of his old friend's death at Anguilla. "Last I checked, your recollection of that particular point in history ain't the clearest," he snapped.

"And I'm the first to say you're right about me memory," confessed the bartender. "But if Bonnie Mary carved that on the sword, then maybe it's something we oughtta be payin' attention to."

"We can go ourselves in the jollyboat," suggested Little Jane. "We'd be able to dart among the rocks fair easy in a small vessel like her. Ain't none of the crewmen got to land on the island. And besides, I'll be safe while you do battle with the *Panacea*. You can pick us up after."

Without waiting for Ishiro's reply, Little Jane tossed a few canteens of fresh water into the boat and began to unhitch the moorings.

Ishiro's eyes went wide at the prospect. "No. It ain't safe. Even I've never walked on the island. What if I can't get back to you? I can't leave you here marooned. Jonesy, talk some sense into her. She's —"

Little Jane hesitated, her hand on the last loop of mooring rope. All her life Ishiro had been the voice of reason in the face of plenty of her parents' questionable schemes. She knew he was wise. "Listen to Ishiro while we're away and do what he tells you." How many times had her parents said that? But her parents weren't here now and the words on the sword burned in her brain, demanding she listen.

"It's all right, Captain Ishiro," piped up a voice from behind the rain barrels. It was Villienne, who as his royal majesty's appointed representative on Smuggler's Bay had the right to eavesdrop on all conversations, as a matter of duty only, of course. "They don't have to go by themselves. I'll go with them. It'll be a splendid adventure."

"I don't suppose you can save someone from drowning with a green lichen tea infusion?" remarked Ishiro sarcastically.

"No, but I can help them. I can … I can swim!" proclaimed Villienne. It was one of those passing fancies that seemed like an excellent idea at the time, but like the smudge-proof ink recipe he once concocted out of highly explosive potassium nitrate, was destined to blow up in his face.

"Well, bully for you," growled Ishiro. "You still ain't leaving. We're going into battle and I'll need a capable surgeon on hand."

Villienne's pale face blanched. "Uh, sir, blood's not really my forte."

"What?" Ishiro demanded, incredulous.

"I tend to swoon at the mere sight of it. Why do you think I never completed my medical training?"

Ishiro shook his head and muttered something untranslatable in Korean.

"And don't forget, Captain, I'm the one with the letter of marque," said Villienne, uncowed. "It's signed by me and I can just as soon revoke it as give it into your power."

"But this — this is insubordination!"

Villienne opened his mouth to argue, but Little Jane stopped him with a tug of his arm. "C'mon, the masthead — it'll be behind us soon."

Jonesy and Little Jane had already loosed the jolly boat's moorings from the deadlights. "Magistrate, come on," insisted Little Jane as she hopped in behind Jonesy.

"My regrets, Ishiro," Villienne said with a sweep of his hat, "but you can court marshal us when we get back to the Bay."

The magistrate put one foot on the gunwale of the boat. It swayed precariously beneath him, but Jonesy grabbed him by the waist and plunked him down safely beside him. Jonesy grabbed a rope and hauled away. Little Jane grasped another, and with a creaking of pulleys they winched the jollyboat down.

As he watched the small boat lurch down the hull of the ship, Ishiro felt his recently renewed strength ebb out

through his fingertips. Of all the heart-wrenching decisions he'd been forced to make in his lifetime, he couldn't
say which was more difficult — choosing to maintain position on the *Newton* against the French fifteen years ago,
knowing the sacrifices he and his men would be forced to
make; or letting Little Jane, the closest thing he had to a
daughter, go off without him by her side to face whatever
unknown dangers might lurk on this mysterious island.

He glanced around, taking in the sudden silence on
the bridge of the *Yorkman*. The crew awaited his orders. *If
only one's feelings were something a man could turn on and
off at will*, he thought, *how much easier life might be.*

But Ishiro let the swell of command overtake him like
a gust of wind, and he thrust his chest forward.

The enemy, he thought grimly, *had best beware.*

Chapter Eight

The Reflection

Long John awoke to the sensation of Bonnie Mary pecking tenderly at his neck. "Not now, love," he whispered. He cracked open one eyelid and yelped. A beady black bird eye in a orange feathered face stared quizzically back at him.

"Shoo!" yelled Long John, swatting the bird away.

"Caw!" cried the bird, its long, narrow beak the colour of a ripe tangerine.

"That's right, you filthy fowl. That's what you get when ye mess with Captain Long John Silver!" he growled, shaking his fist as it flapped away. He half expected someone to laugh at this, but the camp was silent except for various noises related to urgent, painful calls of nature. The previous night's dinner of barbequed orange bird meat had done its dastardly work.

With such unpleasant sounds surrounding him, Long John doubted he'd be able to fall asleep again. He grabbed his crutches, which Darsa had grudgingly returned to him the night before, and pushed himself up. He struggled over to a nearby rock, where he sat down to take stock of his condition. His entire body was covered in maddeningly itchy mosquito bites and his hands were cut up from the previous day's climb. Experimentally, he prodded his broken knee. He gasped as it throbbed painfully against the restraints of the splint.

Leaning heavily on the crutches, Long John rose and made for the moat, weaving his weary way through the pirate hunters' camp. At the water's edge, he gingerly lowered himself down onto the black sand and splashed some of the cool water onto his sunburned face.

To his astonishment, as he looked down into the water, he saw the face of his father, Long John Silver the First, staring back at him. He recoiled from the spectre, heart knocking against his ribs.

As his heart steadied itself, he leaned carefully out over the water, forcing himself to close his eyes first before looking down again. Ah, now he saw the trick of it. It was just his reflection; the cobwebs of sleep mucking with his mind. Of course it wasn't *him*. He thought it funny that the vision had surprised him. As if he hadn't made his fortune off the similarity all those years.

Oddly enough though, Jim had never noticed any physical resemblance between himself and his father, but suddenly here it was. Now ancient, half-remembered conversations slithered up from the depths of his distracted brain, like hidden worms wriggling to the surface after a rainstorm.

Long John Silver — the *real* Long John Silver — rose up before him as mockingly tall and fierce as he'd ever been in life. What would he think of his namesake if he were to see him now? Jim could imagine only too well.

Jim studied his worn-out reflection. What a picture! So hard to believe he'd been thought of as quite handsome back in the tender days of his youth. His now balding head had once sprouted a thick bloom of yellow curls, and his eyes had been startlingly blue and bright. He'd had fine white teeth and an easy smile, not to mention a certain fondness for flash clothing, still not entirely dispelled by age. As a child, the women of the island loved to indulge him. He'd grown up a keen flirt, able to make any of them laugh with his clever stories.

He had fond memories of strolling down the dirt road, scuffing up clouds of yellow dust as he went, listening to the island birds singing in the trees overhead, on his way to the market. He'd often stop for a spell to shoot the breeze with the sailors' wives working in their gardens, everyone eager to stop their digging and say "good day," sweet mangoes exchanged for the latest gossip from the tavern.

Though his gait was never even, he didn't limp. "Nah, not him," they used to say, "that boy, he *swagger.*"

And why not? Smuggler's Bay was *his* then; the little prince of the island he was. The name Silver meant power on Smuggler's Bay and everyone knew it. They let Jim get away with mischief children of their own would've been whipped for, and he never thought that anywhere else in the world could be any different. He assumed that life off-island would be just as simple — that he would always be able to charm his way through.

The only person seemingly immune to young Jim's charm was Long John Silver the First. Jim had always been somewhat frightened of the "original silver-tongued devil hisself," as his mother styled him. He could never picture his father without his crutch beside him. He looked down at the crutches that lay at his side. *Sticks or no sticks, you ain't the same sort of man as him at all*, he told himself.

But was it true?

In the hazy half-light of the morning, Jim sat on the black sand, seeing another beach in his mind's eye, the one in Smuggler's Bay as it'd been when he was young.

He remembered working one day alongside his father's crew, helping prepare the ship for another of its innumerable smuggling runs. By the time he returned to the docks he was exhausted, hands heavy as iron weights by his sides.

But then he saw the sea, blue and sparkling beyond the beach. Instantly refreshed, he went down to examine the gifts left by the retreating tide.

All fatigue forgotten, he darted around like a speedy minnow, peeking into tidal pools and poking at the jellies, remaining at nothing for more than a few minutes at a time.

Old Captain Silver followed Jim down; happy to set his own slow, relaxed pace. He sat on a big sun-warmed rock like a wrinkled old basking turtle, eyes closed, more power in his stillness than in all young Jim's frenzied motion.

Finally, the old captain cracked open an irritated eye. "Sit down," he ordered Jim in his great booming voice, "You need your queue fixed."

The sun was sinking lower, throwing an orange glow across the water, and though Jim wanted to go looking for crabs while it was still light, one didn't match words with the Captain. He plopped himself down on the sand at the base of the rock to let his father braid his hair.

He watched the sun's broken reflection skip across the water, praying his father hadn't noticed the recent disappearance of his third-favourite pipe and snuff pouch.

Captain Silver's tough old hands unwound Jim's hair and split the golden strands into three, weaving them into a flawlessly taut braid. Trying to ignore the sensation of each pulled hair straining to stay rooted to his scalp, Jim played with the sand.

"You know I been talking to some of them old fisher fellows down by the cove," rumbled his father as he brought out a scrap of black leather to bind the queue. "Says you been helping them out with the nets of late."

"Yes, sir." He tried to keep his tone as neutral as possible, unsure of which way his father would tack in the conversation.

"Ol' Leland, he tells me we'll make a fair sailor of ye yet."

"Really?" asked Jim eagerly, all caution forgotten. "He say that, true?"

"Aye, he do." A thoughtful look stole over Captain Silver's craggy features as he finished tying off the queue. "Ain't you going to ask what I tells him back?"

"What'd you tell him?" asked Jim, turning to look at his father.

The captain said nothing at first, only sucked on his pipe, but Jim knew to wait. Nervously, he brought the small pile of sand between his legs into a perfect right angle triangle. He felt a budding navigator's delight in the precision of his creation.

Old Captain Silver tapped his pipe out on the rock. "I tells him he were right …"

For a moment Jim glowed with pride, but then his father continued.

"You *would* make a capital sailor, on'y it weren't for one thing."

Jim glanced down at the perfect ninety-degree angle of his triangle, which he'd been so pleased with a second ago, and knew it'd only come out so well because one of its sides was as straight as the measuring ruler in his navigation kit. And just as wooden. He blushed as he rubbed the triangle away. "I gets by a'right," he mumbled.

"Aw now, you fretting on that little bit of timber of yours there?" his father chuckled.

Jim's face grew hotter, but he didn't look up.

"I seen men do a lot more with a lot less." The captain laughed and slapped his own truncated thigh. It was cut off too high for him to even wear a wooden leg. "T'ain't that what's holding you back."

"Don't I know me maps, compass, sextant, angles, and backstaffs proper? If it ain't that, then what be wrong?"

"What be wrong," repeated the old Captain, stroking his upper lip, "is that yer too damned soft, I says to him.

Too damn soft by half."

"Soft?" Jim asked, confused. He looked down at his hands, calloused hard and tough as any grown seaman's. The skin was so thick on his palms that he could pierce it with a needle and feel only the faintest pinprick.

Old Silver laughed from deep in his belly. "It ain't your hands what's soft, Jim. It's in here," he added, poking the boy's narrow chest with a thick finger. "Yer soft in here, me lad, and ain't no amount o' navigator's know-how can do a thing about *that*."

"Is that a fact?" asked Jim tartly.

"That's a fact," said his father as he brushed the pipe ash off his hands. "Yer a good boy, Jim, and a helpful lad to yer mum down the pub, but yer problem is you thinks all them others is good and helpful as you. That ain't what the world's about, me boy. Outside this island there ain't no one to help you. You see me life? The life a seaman leads? It ain't no life for soft-hearted chaps."

"I ain't no soft-hearted —" Jim began indignantly.

"The sea's broken plenty o' tougher nuts than you, lad," Old Silver scoffed. "I been around a long time. Trust me, I knows."

"No you don't!" Jim's voice rose in unaccustomed anger. Nobody ever yelled at the Captain, but Jim could no longer hold back. He tried to rise, but his father's powerful hands were at his shoulders, pushing him back down with no outward sign of effort.

"Now you sits and listens, Jim. You ain't a littl'un no more, and this here world ain't all fairy stories like your mum done tol' you. You want to go out and you want to survive, you want to be a leader of men, you gets *wise*, lad, you gets wise. You get wise to the evil ways of other men, or you die. Simple as that."

"And what if they're not all evil?"

"When the chips're down and survival's at stake, they *are*, Jim. Time you learned t'keep yer own council and trust no one but yerself …"

Jim was staring so intently at his father's face as he spoke, he didn't notice what the old man was doing with the rest of his body. With the boy still unaware, old Captain Silver slyly hooked the tip of his boot under Jim's bottom.

Before he knew what was happening, the startled boy was tumbling head over heels down the beach, where he landed with a splash in the water.

Sitting on his rear end in the shallows, he shook himself out like a stunned dog and spat out the salty water. Somehow he found his footing and struggled his soggy way out of the sea, before any big waves came to pull him under.

On the sand he stopped to pull off a piece of kelp tangled around his peg leg. Water sloshed around inside. He'd be waterlogged for days now, he thought angrily.

"Atta boy!" cried the captain, clapping his hands together. "You gets tough and watch out for the other fella!" He laughed. "You watch yer back, Jim, 'cause if you don't learn to use the other man first, you best be sure *he's* gonna learn to use *you*."

Jim clenched his fists as he squelched up the beach, forgetting he was still carrying the piece of kelp. As he stomped up to his father's rock, he thought of all the choice things he would say to him. The captain was still laughing, eyes closed and mouth wide open. Then Jim realized he really had nothing more to say. All he could do was fling the soggy piece of kelp straight at his father's big laughing mouth.

"Hope ye choke on it!" he shouted as he darted out of the old man's reach. His father's wrath was a terrifying thing to be sure. He knew he'd catch it badly for this, but at that moment he didn't care.

Captain Silver spat the sandy piece of kelp out with a grunt. He looked back at Jim with a twinkle in his eye, a wide, knowing grin on his lips. "Atta boy! Looks like you're a mite harder'n Thesely thinks."

"What?" asked Jim. Confusion, hurt, and fury all clambered for attention in his spinning head. He felt another emotion as well — pride. Pride that he'd managed to pull it off. He, Jim Silver, had put one over on the greatest liar the island had ever known. For even then, young as he was, Jim knew his father's first guess had been correct. He *was* soft. This show of toughness was just that, a show.

As the years passed, Jim grew. He learned to haul cannon shot until his biceps were as wide around as the cannon barrel itself, and he lifted crates of cargo until his veins stood out under his skin like rope. He bore the tattoo needle, always sober never drunk, all to prove … *what exactly?* He was dismayed to find himself still no different for any of it. Through it all he remained the same foolishly soft-hearted Jim, no matter how much he altered his exterior.

He'd always known there were certain things — *physical* things — that he couldn't change, work and pray as he might. But things as insubstantial as thoughts and feelings — how could it be that he couldn't change *them*?

Yet somehow he knew it'd be far easier for him to learn to dance a proper sailor's hornpipe than to change that secret part of his nature. Try as he might, he just couldn't stand to hack away that softness inside himself as his father'd told him to. It confounded him why it should be so, but there it was. False as parts of him might always be, and resigned as he was to it, he wouldn't resign himself to life with a wooden *soul*, a dumb placeholder without warmth or feeling where his humanity ought to be.

It was this stubbornly soft part of him that, with time, came to hate certain aspects of his father's business. Even as a child, he noticed people were afraid of Captain Silver in a way they weren't afraid of anyone else. Men claiming to be old acquaintances would turn up at the inn; rough characters, possessed of empty, flat gazes, with nothing moving behind their eyes. There were dark deeds muttered about by drunks when they thought he wasn't around. From them he heard his father had killed on more than one occasion. Not just in the heat of battle, either.

But as Jim grew older he discovered there were other ways to command a ship. After all, Old Silver was only one of many successful pirates and smugglers around. Jim watched Captain Thomas Bright and learned how lightly one could wield power. What to his father's mind would have been seen as weakness, to Captain Bright was financial prudence. Bright was an expert in the art of "the show." Usually his prey surrendered with barely a single volley of ammunition, they appeared so obviously out-matched by his huge ship with its massive cannons. From afar, Bright's enemies had no way of knowing that half his cannons were broken, rusty, out of shot, or filled with soggy powder. All they saw was his overpowering show of arms. Even his trading partners could never guess how skint he often was from his carefully maintained façade of expensive clothes and lavish dinner parties.

It was true, Captain Bright was no gentleman. He stole for a living and lied every day of his life. But even Jim could see Bright was a different breed of pirate than Silver. Ultimately, Jim modelled himself after Bonnie Mary's father rather than his own. Like Bright, Jim only fired his gun in battle, certainly never on an unarmed man. "A true gentleman of fortune should never have to," he had once heard Captain Bright say.

When the time came, Jim had mixed feelings about taking on his father's name. He'd been a mewling infant when Thesely Silver found him, but somehow she'd known him instantly as the son of her soul and took him in without reservations. The Old Captain's true feelings about Jim were always a little harder to fathom. Eventually, though, it seemed he came to trust Jim, to bestow on him his most valuable legacy — his own *name*. How could Jim say no?

After his father's death, Jim began to suspect that Long John the First, that deep, scheme-loving man, had had the last laugh after all, or at least had possessed his own reasons for encouraging Jim to take his name.

He wasn't ruthless, and a pirate needed to be ruthless, Jim knew. That was the *real* reason his father had left the name to him. The name made things easier, no question about it. Jim wasn't forced to earn his reputation through bloody deeds of shocking cruelty like others who flew the black flag. When merchantmen heard the name Silver, they surrendered without a fight.

And now here he was, nearing fifty and *still* living off his father's infamy, willing to profit from deeds he himself disdained. It was a little disgraceful, really. He was too good to fully live up to the name's reputation, yet too bad to forsake it completely.

After all, a fellow *does* need to make a living, he always told himself.

Ordinarily, it was not enough to keep him up at night. Ordinarily though, he was not charged with the task of killing Fetzcaro Madsea, his former best friend, preferably within the next forty-eight hours, if it wasn't too inconvenient.

Fraud, the wind whistling through the cataract between the cliffs whispered. *You're a fraud, Jim Silver. If you was a strong man, you'd already have found a way t' gut him like the bottom-feeding catfish he is.*

Jim ran sweaty fingers through his thinning grey curls, trying to erase the memory of Fetz the way he used to be: the smiling, gap-toothed boy who'd been his friend.

It don't matter what he once was, his father's voice echoed back to him across the years. *You kill him, son. You find a way, or mark me words, he'll kill you.*

This time Jim knew his father was right. *Strong or weak, I will kill Fetz, or die meself by his hand.* No choice in the matter. No choice this time. To defend Little Jane and Bonnie Mary, all was permitted. Fetzcaro Madsea would die.

The sound of boots crunching on black stone gravel behind him startled Jim from his reverie.

"What'd you do to them?" said a hoarse voice at his back. He felt a boney hand at his elbow and the pressure of cold metal between his shoulder blades. Like a genie incanted from the bottle of his own errant thoughts, Madsea was suddenly behind him. "What did you do to them?" he repeated over Long John's shoulder, digging the pistol into his back.

"Do to who now?"

"You poisoned me crew!" snarled Madsea.

"What?"

"You ask me who or what one more time and I'll blow yer block off, ye devil!"

By now Bonnie Mary had rushed up to where they stood. "Stop it, Fetz!" she cried.

"It's those damn birds, ain't it?" murmured the *Panacea*'s captain. "Me men ate the birds and now they're all sick! You tainted the meat. I know you did."

Long John and Bonnie Mary exchanged a look.

"You, Mary." Madsea turned, pointing the muzzle of his gun squarely at Bonnie Mary's chest. "You tell me the truth."

"Fetz, these two ate the birds, too, and look, they're fine," Doc Lewiston broke in as he arrived on the scene. "In fact, you ate the meat yourself and seem none the worse for wear. Let's not be rash now. Perhaps there's some other explanation."

"And you? You ate the birds. How do you feel?" Madsea turned to Lewiston.

"Right as rai —" but before he could finish, poor Doc Lewiston felt something nasty gurgle in his stomach. "Just a moment," he said, before staggering off behind some rocks, where he was violently ill.

Madsea's black eyes glared malevolently at the two pirates, but his voice was calm. "Forget the birds for a second. Why don't you two tell me how you plan for us to cross the moat."

"Well, uh, usually," improvised Bonnie Mary, "we builds us a … raft."

"A raft? With what?" Madsea glanced around the bleak stretch of black sand. There were no trees in sight.

"Usually, see, there's a few pieces of driftwood around," said Bonnie Mary.

"What with only two people, it ain't never been a problem," Long John added. This was a part of the plan they had not considered, having never truly constructed a raft to get across the moat before, but they couldn't let Madsea know that.

"Seems to me," said Bonnie Mary slyly, "your men used all the driftwood they could lay hands on to build that fire last night."

Madsea's eyes blazed like black coals in his bone-white face. "And you never thought to mention this when they were throwing the wood on the fire?"

"I tell you what," said Long John in a conversational tone, "why don't you just relax. Me and Mary, we'll go out and fetch ye some wood. We'll get a raft up and ready for you fellas in no time."

With the pistol still trained on Bonnie Mary, Madsea's hand shook with fury. "Ye take me for daft? You two aren't leaving me sight till my crew's up and well. Understand? And tonight," he roared out to the rest of his party, "tonight we'll all be feasting on hard tack and ship's biscuit. No more of these damned birds. Do I make meself clear?"

A handful of half-hearted "yes sirs" and "ayes" were outnumbered by the indelicate moans of several of the others being sick.

"Oh, buck up!" shouted Madsea as he kicked a rock out across the moat.

No one saw the pebble Madsea kicked into the lagoon deal a glancing blow off the tip of a grey dorsal fin in the water.

Doc Lewiston returned, ashen-faced.

"Oh, it's the birds all right," Madsea said bitterly to the physician. It was a statement, not a question. He transferred his pistol to his left hand and slipped his sword from its sheath with his right. Almost gently, he pressed the sword point into the button of Bonnie Mary's shirt.

"You've been picking up some bad habits, Mary."

"How's that?"

"Jim were always the liar, not you."

"Don't know what you're —"

In that moment, with both Madsea and Lewiston's attention focused on Bonnie Mary, Long John seized his chance. He raised one of the crutches, aiming to bring it down on Madsea's head. He was just a hand span away from cracking Fetz's skull when a hand shot out of nowhere and grabbed his arm.

"Watch out, Captain!"

In a split second, Darsa had twisted Long John's arm behind his back and forced him to the ground.

His knee hit the hard-packed sand, momentarily blinding him with pain. He let out a groan, unable to move.

"Not as fast as you used to be, eh, Jim?" Madsea laughed, his sword still trained on Bonnie Mary, his pistol on Long John. "You ain't got me licked, Jim Silver. Not by a long shot," he crowed. "Whatever's sickened them, it's me and my men what got the arms in this outfit. You try to take us down, trust me, ain't all of them so sick one of 'em won't nail you with a shot or two. You think you're safe because I need you to find the treasure? Pah! I don't need the both of you. And frankly, me one-legged friend, you *are* slowing us down."

Madsea's finger stroked the trigger of the pistol, still aimed at Long John, lying motionless on the ground. Darsa wisely rolled off his foe, not wishing to come between the captain and his wrath.

"Fetz, don't shoot!" Bonnie Mary cried. "It's enough, just leave him be. He can't hurt you now."

"Aye, I do suppose you've got a point there, Mary." Madsea shrugged and lowered the sword, and sliding it back into its sheath. "What's he going to do? Bite me to death?" He nudged Long John with the toe of his boot. The pirate flinched away. "Ha! Didn't think so, mate," said Madsea with a smile. In his sunken-cheeked face it looked more like the dead grin of a skull than that of a living man.

Suddenly, he leapt toward Bonnie Mary and the muzzle of the long-barrelled pistol came to rest at the level of her heart. "*You* on the other hand, I've heard it's awful bad luck keeping a woman aboard ship. And a tricksy one like you could prove *well* dangerous."

Bonnie Mary's face went as white as a sheet. She was a veteran of countless boarding parties and pistol duels, but always she came well-armed, never without a weapon by her side. To face an armed enemy without was unthinkable. Yet here she stood, helpless.

She remembered the sight of her own blood that day at Anguilla … flowing without end, without reason, from the awful rip in her face, her shaking hand blindly reaching out for anything that would staunch the flow …

She trembled uncontrollably.

"Stop! Leave her alone." Jim's voice exploded in the air like cannon fire, dispelling her memories, distracting Madsea.

Long John bowed his head. "Listen to me, Fe—, Captain Madsea. You're right. I admit it. It's the bird flesh."

Madsea's head whipped around. "I knew it."

"Please. Just hear me out. Let me explain," begged Long John. "Anyone who eats the bird flesh and don't eat the green lichen aforehand gets the illness. Now you know, so let Bonnie Mary be."

"Pah!" spat Madsea. "Now what're you talking about? What's this green lichen business?"

"The green stuff," Long John explained wearily. "It's all over the island. You know, them mossy bits on the rocks."

Madsea stared back at him, not comprehending.

"Just let him show you," Bonnie Mary pleaded.

Desperate to make his case, Long John snatched a handful of the stuff off a nearby rock and crawled forward until he was as near to Madsea's boot as he dared. He thrust the hairy green up at him. "See. As you ain't sick yet, I'm guessing you already ate some."

"Hmmmm," muttered Madsea, handing his gun to Darsa. He took the slimy green clump between thumb and forefinger and held it up to the light.

Long John inched toward Bonnie Mary. At last he was able to reach out and touch her hand. She crouched down, laced her fingers through his and squeezed, absorbing a measure of calm from his touch.

Madsea was still scowling. "And how do you know this works?"

"Once, long ago," said Bonnie Mary, "me and Jim came to the island right before a powerful storm blew through the area. It lashed the island so hard we feared for our skins and took ourselves to shelter in one of the caves along the mountain. The moat rose mighty high and wavy, too risky to get ourselves back. We got right hungry, waiting days for the storm to pass. Weren't nothing to eat, just the lichen on the rocks and the walls of the cave, so we ate that. At last the skies cleared, and as we made to leave, what should be outside the cave but one of our little orange friends. So, being right starving, we caught and cooked the bird right then and there, thinking to heck with any sickness we got after. We ate and ate, and when we was full and in our right minds again, we waited, knowing the sickness our rash act would bring upon us. But nothing happened. Not that day or the day after. Me and Jim was just fine, and the only reason we could think of was that it was the lichen what saved us."

"So we figured ourselves out an experiment," continued Long John. "The next year when we was back, we ate some of the lichen again, and then one of the birds, and lo and behold, the illness still didn't come for us."

"So there you have it. The green stuff must have some healthful powers, if it can beat back the bird sickness. We've been eating it regular for years. I suppose you develop a taste for it after a while," Bonnie Mary said with a shrug.

Madsea scowled down at the malodorous plant in his hand. "But why am I not ill? I ate the bird flesh, but I don't remember eating anything half as revolting as this."

Long John could think of no answer, but Bonnie Mary thought she knew the reason. "You and Doc Lewiston drank from the pool on the rock. Maybe that's why you ain't sickened. Doc Lewiston and Darsa had some of it too, and see? They're still well enough to stand."

"By Jove, you're right," marvelled the doctor, now fully recovered from his brief bout of illness.

"So if everyone else eats this, their health will return?" asked Madsea skeptically.

"We don't know," admitted Bonnie Mary. "We ain't never tried eating it *after* the bird meat."

"How long do you suspect they'll continue on ill in this way?" inquired Lewiston with concern.

Another inconclusive shrug, this time from Long John. "It could be hours."

"Or days," said Mary.

"Weeks, I've seen it take with some," remarked Long John.

"A man could die of it, I suppose," Bonnie Mary added.

"And you expect me to wait for days or weeks for them to get better?" cried Madsea.

"What do you propose we do then, Captain?" asked Doc Lewiston. "We can't go on just the four of us. You're in no right shape —"

"*I'm* the captain," Madsea exploded. "*I* decide whether I'm in the right shape or not! Come, you heard what they said about building a raft. We'll use what driftwood we can salvage from the fire. Let the rest of 'em mewl and puke their lives away if they wish. If they miss out on taking the treasure, they don't get a share. The fewer men we have to ferry across, the better."

"It's still dangerous," pleaded Long John. "Captain, you should know that there's sharks in them waters. I seen 'em, just last year. Trust me; you don't want to mess with one of them creatures. Why, back when I was a young lad, I were a-swimming here and a shark come up t'me —"

"Oh, do shut up," snarled Madsea, grabbing his gun back from Darsa and pointing it at the two pirates. "Now make yourself useful, and help us find some more wood."

Chapter Nine

East is East

There is an old saw that says "be careful what you wish for." Sitting in the jollyboat on her way to the Nameless Isle, Little Jane remembered how much she'd wished to be a real grown-up pirate, free from her parents' restrictive rules forever. Now here she was, practically captaining her own ship, with no parents around to tell her what to do and feeling no pleasure in it at all. All she wanted was for things to go back to the way they'd been, when she'd felt protected and safe instead of afraid and alone. More than anything, she wanted to see her parents again. But if she asked for that, who knew in what twisted way fate might answer her.

Only two weeks before it had seemed as if everyone else on board knew what they were doing and that she was the only one without answers. She'd trusted in her parents' superior knowledge, simply assuming they'd get the *Pieces* out of any jam.

So much for that. Her parents couldn't save the *Pieces*. They couldn't even save themselves. And if *they* failed, with all their strength, knowledge, and experience, what chance was there for her?

Just little boats upon the ocean, she thought sadly, *all of us just trying to stay afloat in the storm. Don't matter how practiced the pilot steering, none's guaranteed a safe voyage.*

She knew if she were living in one of Villienne's books, the sky would've gone grey and rainy right about now in accompaniment to her lousy mood; however, it remained solid blue, and oppressively bright. How could such a sunny day be so cheerless?

How stupid she felt for taking so much for granted; assuming her parents and the *Pieces of Eight* would always be there; never guessing a person's body could up and betray them like Ishiro's had done; never suspecting people she'd known for years like Ned could suddenly turn on her. All that had been required to send the whole structure of her life tumbling down like a stack of blocks was a knock to the *Pieces of Eight*. Once Ned Ronk kicked that out of place, everything just started to topple. And even if she got it all back, could she ever feel safe and happy again, now that she knew how easily it could all be taken from her?

All her old fears about Australian alligators, vengeful druids, and transforming trees were patently ridiculous, she realized now. There were real things to be afraid of out there and they were far scarier than those even *her* accomplished imagination could conjure up.

What formerly unshakable thing would see fit to betray her next? She didn't want to think about it. So she tried to focus her wandering mind on Jonesy and Villienne, watching as they rowed, trying in vain to stay in synch with each other, Jonesy swearing as Villienne nearly lost another oar to the pull of the waves. *Please don't ever change.* Her thoughts reached desperately out to them. *I couldn't take it if you were to change, too. Just take me home, jollyboat.* She patted the vessel's wood-keeled side. *I'm half-sick of adventure, unbelievable as it may sound.*

In her mind's eye she could see them all back at the Spyglass, her father whittling away at a block of wood, her mother playing fiddle by the light of the fire, Jonesy behind the bar telling her to …

"Wake up Little Jane!" Jonesy yelled. "Hold fast. We're gonna hit."

Little Jane barely had time to grab onto the sides of the boat before they smashed against a piece of submerged coral with a sickening scrape.

"Blast it!" swore Jonesy as he pushed at the coral with one of the oars, trying to force the jollyboat free. Unfortunately, the sharp coral had pierced straight through the hull and the boat was starting to take on water through the gaping hole. Little Jane, Villienne, and Jonesy scrambled out of the small vessel before it could fill up.

"Little Jane! Villienne! Where're you going?" cried Jonesy as he jumped from the boat, his shirt billowing out like a hot air balloon in the water. "We can't just leave the boat here. How'll we get back?"

"Don't worry," said Villienne, patting the barkeep on the shoulder. "With a hole like that drilled in the hull she'll never make it back to the *Yorkman* anyway."

Jonesy glanced at the rapidly filling boat. "Don't worry?" he muttered incredulously, but Villienne and Little Jane were already heading in the direction of the masthead. With a sigh, Jonesy let go of the jollyboat's painter and started off after the others. Somebody had to make sure those two stayed out of trouble.

Luckily, it was shallow enough that they could walk through the choppy surf and still keep their heads above water. It was a most uncomfortable wade over the spiky, coral encrusted terrain to the jagged black rocks of the Nameless Isle, but it wasn't as if they had a choice.

Finally, they made it to shore, and Little Jane was first to begin the climb upward, taking care not to slip on the water-slicked rocks.

How come when Papa talks about his adventures they always sounds like so much fun? she thought crossly. When *he* told his stories, she never doubted he'd manage to get out of any spot of bother. After all, he was right there in front of her, big as life, telling her about it. Even when he ended up outsmarted, like by that Druid who'd turned him into a tree, his stories always had a way of turning out funny somehow. Things made sense. Things were fair. It wasn't all just a bunch of clueless people stumbling around in the dark looking for some way to save themselves, trying and trying but never getting any closer to their goal, running just to stay in place, with everything so bleedin' chancy you just wanted to go ahead and scream.

Furiously, Little Jane smacked the rock. Impassive stone bit into the still-healing flesh of her palm with a sharp, stinging sensation that instantly brought tears to her eyes and a curse to her lips.

Focus on the task at hand, she heard her mother saying with a disapproving shake of her braids. She kept climbing.

As she pulled herself up over the last rock, the masthead came into sight. It was wedged in the midst of a large mound of smaller rocks. From their careful shape and positioning, Little Jane guessed they were placed there by human hands, rather than by some natural phenomenon.

"What is this?" she asked.

"A cairn," said Jonesy, puffing as he pulled himself up beside her. "I told you Old Captain Bright was buried here!"

"This is it? I always thought it'd be bigger, the way me mum talks about him."

"I'd say he was pretty lucky," piped up Villienne, always willing to share a little knowledge. "I mean, statistically, most pirates survive only a few years and are buried at sea or hung from the gibbet as criminals."

"Thanks." Little Jane shot him an irritated glance. "That really helps."

Villienne flushed and tried to correct himself. "Not that I mean you personally or —"

"Just give me your compass," she said before he managed to embarrass himself further.

Villienne removed his gyroscopic pocket compass and watched the needle dance until the arrow came to rest pointing north.

"If north be that way, than east is this way, in the direction of the cairn," muttered Little Jane to herself. "But that makes no sense, we can't walk through solid rock and there's nowhere else to go from here but back the way we came." Little Jane raised a hand to her eyes and looked east. Squinting against the sun, she saw a sudden a flash of light between two rocks. "Look at that!" She pointed.

"I see it, too. It looks like a path through the rocks," said Villienne.

Little Jane scrambled off in the direction of the opening and the two men did their best to keep up.

"You can't possibly expect me to fit through there," protested Jonesy as they approached the narrow opening. Little Jane passed easily through and took off up the path. The tight passage presented no difficulty for Villienne's weedy scholar's frame either. Jonesy sucked in his gut and followed, wedging himself through the crack in the stones as carefully as he could. Thankfully, the path widened as they made their way along, and soon the magistrate and the barkeep were able to walk side by side.

They had been walking for several sweaty, mosquito-filled hours when Little Jane stopped in her tracks, causing Villienne and Jonesy to nearly plough into her from behind.

"Shhhh!" She held a finger to her lips. "Listen."

Jonesy and Villienne heard an eerie sound, like the creaking of rusty hinges on a door, though there was no building in sight. Little Jane pictured a ghostly haunted gate, swinging lazily back and forth as it hung in midair.

"It might be dangerous. Let me go in first," Jonesy whispered. With worried faces, Little Jane and Villienne let him by.

Jonesy crept around the curving corner of a rock face, with Villienne and Little Jane right behind. The water lay far below them now. They heard the creaking sound again, closer this time. Little Jane could have sworn it was right above her, though she saw nothing unusual.

Clang!

"Jonesy!" Little Jane squealed.

Little Jane jumped around the corner after him, wooden sword brandished high, not knowing what horrible sight might meet her eyes.

"Aaah! Get off'r me, you ghost!" yelled Jonesy as he swatted at the air overhead.

When he realized that his fist was stuck inside a rusty old ship's lantern, he looked at Little Jane and Villienne sheepishly.

"Where'd that come from?" Little Jane asked.

Jonesy pointed up at an old metal ring. A single rusty streak ran down the obsidian rock from it like a dribble of bright orange liquid down a blackboard. The streak formed the shape of an arrow, too precisely delineated to be a coincidence. Villienne voiced what they all were thinking: human hands had purposely formed the symbol.

"I don't understand. It's just a straight drop down from here," puzzled Villienne, looking over the edge.

"Or is it?" asked Little Jane, pointing to another arrow etched into the rocky ground. She got down on her hands and knees to take a closer look. At the edge of the cliff she spied two small metal hooks embedded in the rock. There, dangling from the metal hooks down the side of the cliff was a rope ladder, of the same kind she'd often used to climb up the masts on the *Pieces of Eight*. She pulled at it, expecting it to come apart in her hands like the lantern had, but the hempen material seemed sturdy enough. Hoping the hooks in the rock would hold, Little Jane grabbed the top rung, swung her legs over the side, and started making her way carefully down, only bothering to call out to Villienne and Jonesy when she was at the bottom. Soon all three of them had made it down the ladder.

Little Jane, Villienne, and Jonesy looked out across the wide moat of water and felt their spirits sink. From the distant shore, the dark mountain loomed over them, rising high up into the clouds, looking taller than Little Jane had ever seen it before. "Maybe Melvin's wrong," she said wearily.

Chapter Ten

Crossing the Moat

A haphazard structure of lashed-together driftwood with a pair of uneven crutches for oars, that's all it was. Long John shook his head at their handiwork. Much as he hated the crutches, it galled him sorely to sacrifice the useful implements to such a useless cause. Far worse was Madsea's announcement that he would be left behind.

"Fetz, you can't be serious," Long John pleaded desperately. "What of me wife's honour? It ain't proper to let her alone with three men in a boat."

"Raft, you mean. And he's right, you know," added Doc Lewiston. "Propriety dictates we take him. He is her husband, after all."

"Please, Captain Madsea," sighed Bonnie Mary piteously, "I'd be too shamed to go without him."

At this Madsea threw back his head and laughed until he doubled over coughing. "Oh, come now, that's the best you can do? Poor Mary's *honour?* Why, we all know she don't got no more honour than a dockside jade, ain't that right, Mary?"

Staring daggers at Madsea, Bonnie Mary clutched her hands tightly together to prevent herself from ripping her bodice open on the spot to remove the knife. She longed to eviscerate the contemptuous blackguard where he stood.

"You dare! I'll shut yer gob for you," Long John hissed at Madsea. From his place on the ground he lunged for Madsea's ankles, intending to pull the barnacle-sucking son of a bilge rat down to where he could pummel him into a pleasing pulp.

But it was not to be. With a lazy kick to the pirate's belly, Kingly easily intercepted him. Long John grunted but did not stop talking. "Listen," he gasped. "I'll swim you across. I swim like a bleeding otter, I do. Just let me stay with Mary and I'll drag you and your fellows behind me."

"Ah, Jim." Madsea gave a disdainful shake of his head. "It's too late to change your tune now. Come along, Mary," he said, yanking her toward the raft by the rope that encircled her waist.

Gritting her teeth, Bonnie Mary stumbled after him.

"You'll regret this, all a' you. You ain't through with me yet. If I don' get you, the shark in the moat will. Y'mark me words. I'll send 'im after you, I swear!" Long John shouted as they walked away, Kingly carrying the makeshift raft.

Ignoring the pirate's threatening words, Kingly placed the raft upon the water and helped Madsea, Darsa, Doc Lewiston, and an apprehensive Bonnie Mary onto its rickety boards before pushing it out into the moat with quick thrusts of his giant shoulders. The bosun then hopped on before the water became too deep.

"Keep an eye on him, Snepper," Madsea yelled as the raft bobbed away.

"Aye, Captain!" the seaman shouted from shore.

"Come back you daft fools," Long John called after them. He watched the cobbled-together craft bob off across the water, his sweet Mary staring sorrowfully back at him. "Please," he begged.

The sailors well enough to take notice laughed weakly.

Seaman Snepper sniggered, tightening his grip on Long John's arm. All the pirate could do was watch as the raft moved away, Kingly's powerful arms propelling it toward the far shore.

But it wasn't long before another orange-bird-related cramp struck Seaman Snepper, prompting him to release the pirate to seek relief behind the rocks. He left what he thought was a subdued Long John laying on the black sand, forgetting in his urgency that no one ever managed to subdue a Silver for long.

Long John spotted his chance. Edging forward on his belly, the wily pirate slipped quietly into the moat without attracting any notice. He dove down into the cool water and didn't come up for air again until he was well away from shore.

He surfaced with arms swinging. He swam like mad, trying to catch up with the raft. Just then one of the sailors on the shore took notice of his absence. He heard shouting and the report of guns behind him. Luckily, the orange-bird sickness had left the sailors from the *Panacea* so dizzy they could hardly aim their pistols and soon Long John was out of their range.

He swam with all his might, but the opposite shore remained tantalizingly far away. His injured knee still pained him and he was tiring fast. The initial burst of adrenalin that had propelled him through the water quickly faded, and he cursed himself for forgetting to remove Doc Lewiston's splint before diving in. The weight of the splint dragged on him, slowing his progress with every kick. Gritting his teeth against the pain, he managed to pull it off and shake himself free.

Now all he had to worry about were sharks. That is, if there truly were any. Even Long John couldn't be sure if the sharks were just another one of those legends and rumours that tended to collect around the subject of the Nameless Isle, or if they really existed.

Keeping his eyes just above the waterline, he could see the raft bobbing ahead of him. He could have spotted Bonnie Mary's bright orange head-kerchief from a mile away. He didn't want to get too close, as he knew Madsea, Kingly, and Darsa were toting weapons and wouldn't hesitate to shoot him dead in the water if given the chance. Luckily, the small waves making their way across the surface of the water and the sun in their eyes prevented Madsea and his crew from spotting him. And if Bonnie Mary noticed Long John tailing the raft, she obviously said nothing about it to her captors.

Hold fast Mary, he thought. *I'm coming!*

Kingly pulled on his "oar," which was really just one of the crutches wrapped in a seaman's jacket, and looked back toward the shore.

"Haven't they hit him yet?" muttered Madsea in frustration, squinting against the sun.

"No idea, sir," answered Darsa, looking over the water's rippling surface. "Twits couldn't hit the right side of a barn, y'ask me."

Bonnie Mary shaded her eye with her hand, not trusting herself to look directly at the water. She did not want the others to notice if she happened to spot her husband. The gunfire continued, without any telltale cheers to indicate success.

"I'd say Silver's either drowned or out of range by now," Kingly announced sourly.

"Blast!" growled Madsea.

"And he ain't the only one what's following us," added Darsa.

"What? Who else could be out there?"

"*That!*" cried Darsa in alarm. He pointed a shaking finger at a large, shadowy shape in the water. "What in the world is that?"

The other occupants of the raft craned to get a better look. Suddenly, a large grey shape broke the surface of the water just a few feet from the raft. Just as quickly it sank back under. Beneath them something was stirring up the muck at the bottom of the moat. Their eyes darted frantically across the surrounding water. In mute horror, they watched as the grey shape reappeared, circling the raft just below the surface, closer, and closer still. It was heading right toward them.

"Maybe we was wrong before," said Little Jane as they stood at the edge of the moat. There were rocks to the right of them, rocks to the left of them, and a wide moat of water in front of them. From the distant shore, the black cone of the volcanic mountain rose high up into the clouds, taller than anything Little Jane had ever seen.

"So," mused Jonesy. "What do we do now? Melvin got any more bright ideas?"

"We could swim," suggested Little Jane.

"You know I can't swim a lick," admonished Jonesy.

"Then me'n Villienne'll have to do it without you," decided Little Jane. "It's the only way I see we be getting across."

"We can go back and wait for Ishiro to return. We don't have to do this."

"*We* don't," insisted Little Jane, "but *I* do."

"Magistrate." Jonesy looked helplessly at Villienne. "Explain to her why she's wrong."

"Actually, I think she's right," confessed Villienne. "It doesn't look too deep from here. I think we're meant to wade across. The arrow pointed this way. Logically, it can only mean others must have crossed here before."

"Or we could just be completely off the mark," retorted Jonesy.

"Well, I fer one ain't going back!" declared Little Jane. And without further ado she waded into the shallows.

"Villienne, tell her she can't," cried Jonesy, but the magistrate only gave him a sympathetic shrug and began removing his shoes.

Anxiously, Jonesy watched Little Jane wade in up to her waist.

"C'mon, slowcoach, it's nice n' warm!" Little Jane shouted back at Villienne.

"Coming, coming," replied Villienne, stashing his shoes in his knapsack with the specimen jars.

Jonesy cursed his cowardice, but still could not bring himself to enter the water.

"Look out for her, Villienne," Jonesy advised the magistrate, as Villienne waded in.

"Of course, my good man," Villienne reassured Jonesy airily. "I won't let anything happen to her."

"What about sharks?" Jonesy offered feebly.

"Ecologically impossible in water this shallow," Villienne answered cheerfully. "Buck up, Mr. Jones. We'll be fine."

After twenty minutes, Villienne was beginning to feel a little less certain about the "ecological impossibility" of sharks due to the depth of the moat water. The water was now up to his chest, and much murkier. Whenever he stepped down, clouds of mud swirled up in his wake, obscuring the bottom of the moat. If some bloodthirsty creature was swimming around down there, he'd have no way of knowing until it was too late. And if there was one thing more disconcerting to Villienne than anything else in the world, it was not knowing something.

Chapter Eleven

Attack of the *Yorkman*

Lieutenant Jesper paced the deck of the *Panacea*, exuding his characteristic air of jumpy watchfulness. He chewed on a coffee bean, tasting the bitter juice. It was a habit he'd picked up from some Colombian sailors. They told him the beans kept one from nodding off during long night watches, but more importantly in Jesper's case they gave him something to occupy his mouth with. He needed *something* to prevent himself from telling off his listless crew. He knew they couldn't help feeling poorly, but nothing aboard ship was getting done. The cannons were still not primed and the navigational calculations they needed for their return trip were incomplete. Even the boards of the deck hadn't been swabbed and were all sticky, he noticed with disgust.

Captain Madsea survives and comes back, he'll have my head. How did everything get so buggered up so quickly? Jesper wondered as another intestinal cramp tore through him and he was forced to take refuge in the water closet used by the common crew. He left the bridge against his better judgement, hoping all hell wouldn't break loose in the interim.

Unaware of the trouble on board the *Panacea,* the *Yorkman* glided smoothly around the coast of the island, while down in the hold the men prepared for the sneak attack. A hand signal from the crow's nest confirmed what Captain Ishiro had already seen with his own eyes. They were almost upon the enemy ship.

The men pulled on the ropes to hold the sails of the *Yorkman* taut, preventing them from luffing noisily in the breeze. All commands were issued through hand signals rather than the customary shouts and even Captain Ishiro's nominal officers took off their shoes, so as not to make any noise walking upon the deck.

To be truthful, Ishiro was astounded they'd managed to get this close without the *Panacea*'s lookouts spotting them. Peering through his spyglass, he was puzzled as to why he could see no hands holding down the posts at the forecastle, helm, and wheel. Then the wind shifted and the putrid air emanating from the Panacea wafted over the *Yorkman*'s bridge, nearly choking Ishiro with its stench where he stood. Even perpetually unwashed sailors grimaced, disgusted at the pungent aroma. Ishiro felt his spirits rise as he realized just exactly what the *Panacea*'s crew must have been eating. As they sailed silently closer to the *Panacea*, Ishiro was pleased to note that the only sailors moving about on the deck of the enemy ship were those formerly of the *Pieces of Eight*. Maybe their luck was finally changing.

Hold fast, mates. Ishiro smiled at the sight of his former shipmates, all upright, and in perfect health for helping the invasion. *Won't be long now.*

"On my signal," he whispered to Matan, the cannon master, as he held up his hand.

The hands at the cannons made a few last-minute adjustments as the *Yorkman* glided still closer to the reeking *Panacea*.

Just a little bit more.

They were so close now that any word uttered on the *Yorkman* could be distinctly heard on the *Panacea*. Still, no one on board the enemy vessel seemed to take notice of their approach. Ishiro brought down his hand, the sign for the cannon master to order the gunners to fire. The fuses of the cannons were lit just as the first cry of alarm came down from the mizzenmast of the *Panacea*. The *Yorkman* was spotted at last, but too late to do the crew of the *Panacea* any good. The cannonballs quickened in their well-greased wombs. Fuses burned quickly down to the metal and the air exploded in a volley of cannon fire.

Lieutenant Jesper was just emerging from below decks as the first volley of enemy fire arched over his bridge.

On the *Yorkman*, Ishiro was close enough to hear the sounds of splintering wood and angry commands that came too late. He prayed his friends remained unharmed as he gave the signal for another volley. The recoil from so much simultaneous firing sent the iron cannon barrels bucking back like startled horses under the gunners' hands. Frantically they sponged the cannons down and prepared to fire again.

At last the gun deck of the *Panacea* roared to life, but the use of cheap, inferior powder and the lack of healthy men to service the cannons provided insurmountable problems. As a result, the *Panacea*'s response was a lacklustre, uncoordinated volley. Most of the *Panacea*'s cannonballs sank harmlessly into the water between the two ships. The few shots that did manage to hit the *Yorkman* met a new type of hull constructed of sturdy live oak. The shots bounced right off her with barely a scratch.

As the smoke cleared, Ishiro spied a gaping hole in the *Panacea*'s belly. A cheer rose up from the deck of the *Yorkman* as the rest of the crew spotted it.

A hit!" shouted Ishiro gleefully, with a sudden rush of relief. "A most palpable hit!"

"Hold fast, men!" Madsea screamed.

Bonnie Mary dug her fingers into the gaps between the lashed-together pieces of driftwood as the sinister fin sliced through the water. She expected the shark to take the craft in its massive jaws and tear it to shreds. Instead, the grey fin disappeared beneath the raft again. Heart knocking at her ribs, Bonnie Mary surveyed the water for any sign of the creature's presence, but the wind had died down and the surface was now eerily still. For a few tense seconds she waited, listening to the ragged breathing of Madsea over the loud rush of blood in her ears, every fibre of her body as taut as a tightened wire.

Suddenly, there was a loud crack. The shark was ramming them from below. As her companions screamed, she felt the timbers of the raft shiver as the creature continued its assault. She glanced from the disintegrating raft beneath her to the distant shore and back again. *Where to go?* She couldn't swim, but she couldn't just sit there as the raft was smashed to bits.

Instantly, one sickening blow from the creature stripped her of all choice. With another ear-splitting crack the raft splintered into a thousand pieces. Bonnie Mary felt herself catapulted through the air at an alarming speed, the captain, doctor, bosun, and steward close at her heels.

Before she could fully comprehend what was happening, she landed with a splash back in the water, pieces of the ruined raft raining down around her.

Panicked, she flailed around, attempting to recall the details of an aborted swimming lesson Jim had given her years before. Then, just as she was slipping below the surface, one of her desperately windmilling arms connected with something hard bobbing on the surface. Immediately, she felt herself rising back up. As she surfaced, she heard splashing and the sound of male voices cursing and sputtering, but they sounded far away.

Her hair was tangled around her face. She managed to shake it away enough to breath easier without releasing the object keeping her afloat, but her eyes stung from the salty water and she could not see very well.

She turned in what she hoped was the direction of shore and desperately started kicking her feet.

"Ahoy there, mate!" cried out a friendly voice.

"Jim?" she cried in disbelief. She released one hand from her floatation device to flip her tangle of braids away at last. By some miracle, there he was swimming toward her.

"You all right?" he called out as he drew closer.

Bonnie Mary nodded, rubbing the salt water from her stinging eyes. "You?"

"Ain't shot yet," he said with a wan smile.

Then she remembered the creature, still at large in the water. "There's a shark!" she warned him. "Be careful!"

"It's well away from us now," he said as he drew up to her, strong arms treading the surface. "It seems to like its entertainment elsewhere, anyway." Before Bonnie Mary had a chance to ask him what he meant by that, she heard him chuckle.

"Well bless me soul," he exclaimed as he touched the floating piece of wood in her hands. "Look what you found!"

She looked down and laughed, realizing that the floating piece of wood she'd managed to grab hold of was one of his crutches, last seen in use as a raft oar.

"Thought I'd hang onto it for you," she told him, smiling.

Long John kissed her on her salty mouth and together, holding the makeshift flotation device in front of them, they kicked their legs, making for the distant shore of black sand.

"What of the others?" Bonnie Mary asked as they went, thinking how she'd hate to see Doc Lewiston drown. He'd been nothing but kind to them despite his position.

"Lucky sods're all hanging on to the remains of the raft." Long John slipped her a crafty smile. "All except one." He nodded his head toward the area of the moat they'd just left and Bonnie Mary turned to witness something truly startling.

As she watched, she saw the shark leap out of the water, flipping in an easy backward arc, as if it did that sort of thing every day. In that instant she recognized the "shark" for what it truly was: a dolphin!

Now some folks, at a moment like that, would say to themselves: *Phtt! A dolphin? We got all worked up over a dolphin?* But not Bonnie Mary. Ever since she'd seen a dolphin pod tear a massive great white shark into a pulpy mass of chum after it dared threaten one of their young, she'd always treated the species with respect. After all, seven feet of highly intelligent, hydrodynamic muscle in a bad mood is not something to dismiss lightly.

As if seeking to prove her sentiments, the cetacean stood upon its tail flukes balancing a white-faced Fetzcaro Madsea on its snout. As the two pirates watched, the creature flipped the *Panacea's* captain up in the air, caught him, and bounced him off its snout again like a rubber ball, all the while making strange clicking noises. Had Bonnie Mary not known better, she could have sworn the creature was laughing.

As the dolphin threw Madsea up again, light as a rag doll, Long John grinned. This time the creature tossed Madsea way up, too far and too high to catch. The captain landed with a sickening splash right in front of Long John and Bonnie Mary.

In a fog of terror, Madsea thrashed in the water, reaching out for whatever he could grab hold of. What he could grab hold of, it turned out, was the waterlogged crutch. With a drowning man's frenzied strength he wrenched the piece of wood away from a surprised Bonnie Mary. Unfortunately, the spindly crutch was long past being an adequate flotation device, soaked through as it was. Madsea began to sink.

Down, down, down he went.

But, luckily for him the last *down* was a rather short one. In fact, Madsea suddenly realized, as his backside hit the sandy bottom, that he was hardly down far at all. Abruptly, he gathered his feet under him and stood up. The water reached just above his chest.

Giggling breathlessly with relief, he took one step, then another. Soon the water was at his waist. Looking up ahead, he could see Jim and Mary scrambling up the bank, heading for the mountain as fast as their exhausted bodies could carry them, which, with Bonnie Mary supporting an injured Jim, was not very fast at all.

Madsea heard the angry clicking sounds of the dolphin behind him. Suddenly, he felt as if he had been punched in the calves. The dolphin nearly knocked Madsea off his feet with its powerful snout, but he managed to stay upright and slog his way through the shallows without the vengeful creature attacking him any further. He made it to the black beach at last and stumbled onto the rock-strewn sand. Spotting Long John and Bonnie

Mary limping along up ahead, he slung the much-abused crutch over his shoulder like a club and grinned. They would be easy prey.

But just as this happy thought came to mind, Madsea heard a loud boom. Madsea instantly recognized the sound of distant cannon fire and had the sinking feeling that the *Panacea* was under attack.

Not being well-versed in the art of silent meditation, Jonesy quickly grew bored waiting for Little Jane and Villienne to return.

He had never been the type of man content to hang back while his friends and family placed themselves in peril. Yet without the ability to swim the moat, what use was he to them? Without a clear answer to this question, Jonesy headed off down the narrow strip of black sand to see what he could find.

After walking for about a quarter of an hour, he spied several shapes in the distance. Using his spyglass he noted about a half-dozen sailors lying in varying positions of abject wretchedness on the sand. These men, Jonesy assumed, were the remains of the *Panacea's* landing party, though he figured there had to be more than these few sickly specimens. Maybe the ones who were healthy enough had continued on. Still, in time even these fellows, ill as they were, could make trouble for Little Jane and Villienne.

Well, thought Jonesy, *least I could do is try to make some trouble for them in return.*

He sank to a crouch and made his way up and away from the water, where it was rockier and the scrubby vegetation encroached upon the sand. Here he could approach the men without being spotted. With his fighting knife in one hand (the pistol he'd brought had been lost when they'd run aground) and a large rock in the other, he approached the unsuspecting sailors. The first man he came upon was lying face down on the sand, groaning as he clutched his stomach. Jonesy immediately fell upon him. He managed to subdue the weakened fellow with little resistance, but the sailor's cries quickly roused the others from their lethargy.

"Murderer!" came a full-throated shout from one of the other men.

"No! No!" protested Jonesy, visions of a return to Newgate Prison clouding his mind. "I ain't. I swears it. See." He held up his victim by the collar. The man blinked stupidly in the sunlight. "See? I just stunned 'im. He'll be all right in a tic. Ain't that so, mate?" Jonesy asked him.

But the barkeep's mercy toward their comrade did little to appease the other sailors. They screamed in rage and thundered toward him, swords drawn.

Jonesy swore briefly before dropping the man and turning to flee from the onslaught of enraged sailors. Just then, from beyond the ring of rocks, came the unmistakable sound of cannon fire. Instantly distracted from the chase, the sailors stopped in their tracks and looked at one another.

"What was that?"

"Look. Smoke. Someone's attacking the ship!"

"Forget him. All hands back to the *Panacea*. On the double!"

And with that the sailors turned and ran up the beach, scrambling over the rocks, off to defend their beleaguered ship.

Jonesy stood up and blinked, suddenly alone on the beach. Even the sailor he'd stunned had somehow managed to stumble off in the general direction of the cannon fire. It had all happened in a matter of seconds. Jonesy looked down at the scattered supplies they had left behind them on the sand. The campsite was littered with shirts, shoes, tents, pots, and cooking utensils. There was something else, too. With a gleam in his eye, he reached down and picked up a pistol.

Chapter Twelve

All Hands on Deck

Ned Ronk looked around the smoking deck of the *Panacea* in dismay. A few panicked sailors were running to belatedly load their weapons and fire the rest of the cannons. Anyone could see it was too little, too late.

Lieutenant Jesper ran past Ned, yelling and waving his sword. "What're you standing there for? All hands on deck! Attack!" Jesper screamed at the boatswain's mate, still curled over the scuppers in the throes of orange bird malaise. "You! Man your battle station!"

The weaponsmaster's boy scurried by, handing out arms. Ned gave the inscription on his gun a dubious glance. Who'd ever heard of a *Backer* rifle?

"Look!" someone shouted.

Ned turned just in time to witness Lancashire, Levittson, and Dvorjack attack the *Panacea*'s cannon gunners on the gun deck. In the melee, a pile of cannonballs was knocked from its pyramid formation. The heavy balls rolled down to the lower decks, knocking confused crew-members off their feet as they went.

"Somebody shoot them," screamed Lieutenant Jesper, stamping his foot. "Shoot the prisoners!"

Ned Ronk and seven other men well enough to shoot primed their weapons. Ned had difficulty loading his pistol, as if the chamber was the wrong size for the bullets ...

With a mighty heave, Lancashire broke the harness of the biggest cannon on the ship and sent it hurtling through the railing and into the sea. This was not as hard to accomplish as one might think, for over the past week the crew of the *Pieces* had secretly been taking turns loosening the bolts and thinning the ropes that held the mighty cannons in place. Following the larger man's example, Lockheed and Levittson got behind a pair of 24-pounders and began to push.

"Shoot!" came the order for the riflemen.

Eight bullets bounced into their chambers at once. Eight guns exploded. Eight men fell to the deck, dropping their defective pistols, holding their right hands in agony.

Ned Ronk howled in pain as he rolled on the deck, clutching his burnt hand. The scent of singed flesh and cordite wafted through the air. From somewhere he heard Lieutenant Jesper screaming at another group of sailors to "look lively!"

Freed prisoners helped the other captured crewmem-bers of the *Pieces of Eight* escape their bonds. Together they sent the rest the *Panacea*'s arsenal flying into the sea.

Ned looked up from his scorched hand just long enough to see Lieutenant Jesper fall to the deck in front of him with a thump. The smoke cleared to reveal the *Pieces of Eight's* weaponsmaster, Jezebel Mendoza, crouched over him, in the process of relieving the senseless man of his sword. Beside Jezebel stood the former cabin boy, Rufus, holding a sturdy belaying pin at the ready should Jesper try to rise. Mendoza stood up, the lieutenant's rapier now held in her appreciative grasp.

"A fine addition to my collection," she pronounced. Then she bent into an elegant dancer's plié and extended the sword, flexing the weapon with deadly precision straight at Ned. She favoured him with a predatory smile.

"En garde," she said.

Ned Ronk blinked at her, turned, and, shouldering terrified sailors aside as he ran, barrelled through the chaos of the upper decks.

Weaponsmaster Mendoza looked down at the men still rolling around on the deck clutching their injured hands and shook her head in disappointment. "See, Rufus, no good ever comes of using replicas. Always, *always* insist on the real thing."

Rat in human shape as Ned was, he instinctively realized the moment to abandon ship had come. He wondered where that idiot Madsea was in all this — still looking for his legendary treasure, no doubt. *That blasted treasure!* Now that the *Yorkman* had bested the *Panacea*, Ned knew he'd never see so much as a brass farthing of it.

He decided stubbornly as he climbed over the rail that the treasure would be his. It was only fair. He was the one who had sacrificed his name and position for it. It was time he took fate into his own hands. This resolution set firmly in his mind, Ned pinched his nose and took a deep breath. Then, for the second time in less than two weeks, Ned Ronk jumped ship.

Chapter Thirteen

How to Walk on Water
(and Other Unexpected Skills)

Back on the *Yorkman*, Ishiro urged his men forward. "Quickly," he cried, "before they get to their guns. Let 'er have it on the broadside before she comes about. Don't wait till the smoke clears. Just aim where you was aiming before. One … two … three …" Ishiro brought his sword down as a signal.

"Fire as you bear!" cried the quartermaster.

The second series of fuses were lit. Wicks of kerosene-soaked rope burned for a moment and then …

Booooommmmm!

Thunder exploded outward as the recoil sent the cannons bucking back. The cannonballs flew through the haze of smoke, hitting with uncharacteristic precision at such close range. The crew of the *Yorkman* tensed again, preparing for a third volley.

"One more time, Capt'n?" Matan asked.

But this time Ishiro didn't give the sign. He paused, listening.

"Hold your fire!" he yelled.

Sounds of a scuffle were coming from the *Panacea*, but the smoke was still too thick to see exactly what was happening.

Then they heard another sound.

"We surrender," a high treble voice shouted out across the water. Ishiro thought he recognized it.

"Now *you* say it," the familiar voice on the enemy ship prompted.

Through the smoke came another, deeper voice, off the deck of the *Panacea*. It was Lieutenant Jesper. "We surrender," he said hollowly.

"Louder," ordered the high voice.

"Ouch! Would you stop that," muttered a perturbed Lieutenant Jesper. "Fine. We surrender," he yelled loudly. "Satisfied?"

But his last word was drowned out by the combined cheers of the remains of the *Pieces of Eight*'s crew on the *Panacea* and the crew on board the *Yorkman*.

High above the smoke, a white flag of surrender leapt up the defeated *Panacea*'s mizzenmast. There was a sudden gust of wind, and the smoke cleared enough that Captain Ishiro could make out the figure of Jezebel Mendoza waving at him from the deck of the *Panacea*. Her other hand held the point of a sword to Lieutenant Jesper's throat. Next to her stood Rufus, his trusty belaying pin at the ready. Lockheed motioned enthusiastically from behind the shattered railing of the gun deck, where the *Panacea*'s deadliest cannon had disappeared moments before.

"Ahoy there," cried out Changez, waving his arms like a windmill. "Who goes there?"

"It's Ishiro!" shouted Sharpeye Sharpova, who could always tell this sort of thing, even without a spyglass.

"Good afternoon, *Panacea*. Is everyone aboard shipshape?" Ishiro called from the *Yorkman*.

"Aye-aye!" cried Mendoza. "The hold is filling with water, so we need to get everyone off the ship."

Members of the crew were still making their way up on deck. Thankfully, the former crew of the *Pieces of Eight* all appeared unharmed.

"Good work!" exclaimed the delighted Captain Ishiro. "Wonderful."

"Wonderful? Wonderful, he says? It ain't bleedin' wonderful!" screamed a petulant Lieutenant Jesper at his men, unleashing a litany of curses upon them. "We're sinking, and it's all your fault."

The *Panacea*'s injured shooters glanced up angrily from where they were busy cooling their hands in the ship's mop buckets to mutter some unkind things about their commander.

Before the angry sailors could take any action, however, Ishiro intervened.

"Acting Captain Jesper, I suggest you prepare your men to evacuate ship," he instructed.

"Hurrah! Let's hear it for Captain Ishiro," cried Harley.

Another cheer ran up from the *Yorkman*'s crew, but Ishiro motioned for silence. "Let's wait until everyone's off the *Panacea* before we celebrate. Abandon ship, on the double!"

It is said that into every life, a little rain must fall, mused Doc Lewiston. *Yet no one ever says anything about homicidal dolphins.*

While plenty of exciting things were happening elsewhere, Lewiston was perturbed to find himself suddenly alone, clinging to a piece of the ruined raft for dear life. The current in the moat, which had suddenly become quite strong indeed, was in the process of dragging the good doctor around to the opposite side of the volcano. Though he tried to propel himself toward the nearest shore, his efforts were unsuccessful. He'd never learned to swim, but luckily he was a stout man, with most of his stoutness concentrated in fat, not muscle, and he floated surprisingly well.

Doc Lewiston had almost floated clear around to the other side of the island when one of the peculiar orange birds attracted his attention. Being a medical professional, and a naturally perceptive sort, Doc Lewiston immediately noticed that this bird possessed a remarkable talent. It could walk on water!

Doc Lewiston was still pondering this great scientific discovery as he bobbed closer and closer to the creature. He was on a collision course with the strange bird, but just before they collided, he realized his mistake. The bird wasn't *actually* walking on the water, but on a low rock shelf just under the waterline.

The bird squawked and flapped away as Lewiston was swept straight into the submerged wall of very solid rock. With the wind momentarily knocked out of him, Doc Lewiston let go of the last remains of the shattered raft. With great difficulty, he managed to pull himself up and onto the wall of rock, where he lay gasping for air. When the world came back into focus, he rose to his feet and took stock of his surroundings. Amazed, he saw that the wall of rock seemed to be part of a wider platform of rock, visible just under the surface of the water.

The path appeared to stretch all the way to the interior of the island, over the shore, and up to the base of the cave-dotted mountain. He turned carefully around to look back at the black fangs of rock on the other side and noticed that the barely submerged path continued in that direction, too, all the way to the opposite shore.

Still marvelling at the illusion of walking on water, Doc Lewiston began to edge carefully along the path. He moved in the direction away from the mountain, thinking his best option lay in trying to reach the camp. He knew if he walked all the way around, he could make it back to the other sailors. There he could wait for Madsea and the others to return. The other crewmembers at the camp were still ill with the orange bird malady. If he was not destined to help Madsea, at least he might be able to do something to ease the suffering of the sickly crew.

The water's not getting any shallower, thought Little Jane as she swam. At least it was relatively clear by this point,

providing little cover for sharks or other marine preda-
tors. Realistically she knew, even if she saw a shark coming from far away, it was unlikely she'd be able to swim
fast enough to escape. As for Villienne, he was still walking instead of swimming, though he looked increasingly
uncomfortable as the water continued to rise.

"Come on, it's faster if you swim," she advised him.
"We need t'get to the other side quick as we can."

With the water now up to his shoulders, Villienne
stopped to shift his knapsack to a new position on his
head, where he hoped it might stay at least partially dry.

"Forget yer blasted bag o' jars. We got to get to me
parents afore it's too late." Little Jane glared at him, but
then she noticed something. That look in his eyes wasn't
just worry or discomfort. No, it was an expression of
stark, unreasoning terror at the thought of not being able
to touch the bottom. The true nature of his plight suddenly dawned on her. She cursed herself for not realizing
it before, then cursed him for being fool enough to try it.

"Blast! You can't swim, can you?" She smacked the
water in frustration.

Villienne reared back fearfully as the water hit his
face. Not wanting to trouble anyone with a silly thing
like his imminent drowning, and too proud to admit he'd
exaggerated his talents, he'd tried his best to hide his difficulty for as long as possible.

"Heh," Villienne laughed weakly, "guess you have
me there."

"Let's just hope it don't get any deeper," was all Little
Jane had to say.

But soon the water was too deep for Villienne to walk, and the magistrate struggled to crest even the smallest of waves.

"Look," said Little Jane, trying hard to keep her voice steady. "Stretch your arms like this. See. Watch me. Now kick yer legs. Kick! Kick!" she shouted, but he just sunk farther down in the water.

"Crazy," she spluttered in the salty water. "I don't care that you's a magistrate, why in blazes did you have to go and lie 'bout something as stupid as knowing how to swim?"

"Masthead," gasped Villienne desperately, taking in a mouthful of seawater. "On the *Yorkman* … I knew … knew you … were right. Wanted … wanted to … make sure … sure Ishiro let us go."

"But you could've stayed ashore with Jonesy. You didn't have to …"

She trailed off, aware that Villienne couldn't hear the rest. He was really and truly underwater now and didn't appear to be resurfacing. Little Jane swore, then held her breath and dived down to retrieve him. Grabbing Villienne by his shirt collar, she pulled the sinking magistrate to the surface.

He coughed, spewing up more seawater, while she held him up, trying to make him float as best she could.

"I didn't realize," he gasped, "I thought if *you* could swim, a little girl and all, well, me, a grown man, I should be able to do it easily."

She glared back at him.

"It seemed logical at the time," he protested. "Who thought it'd ever be this hard? I'm so dreadfully sorry.

Now I've spoiled everything," he moaned as he began to slip from her tired arms again.

She spat out a mouthful of saltwater and grabbed at him before he went down again. This sinking tendency of his was beginning to disturb her.

Should they go back? She didn't know if he'd make it. But she couldn't just leave him to drown. It was at this moment that she remembered something her father had taught her that spring in Smuggler's Bay; a way to carry an injured seaman in the water.

He'd discovered it, or so he'd told her, on the Mississippi River, when he saved the life of a wealthy gambler who had been thrown off a steamboat by his sweetheart's jealous suitor. The gambler had repaid Long John with an alligator farm in Florida and a packet of magic orange pips, or so he said. Of course, this being one of her father's stories, who knew what parts, if any, were actually true? Was there a grain of truth anywhere there? He *had* demonstrated the carry to her that day. She prayed that it would work.

"Stop kicking and wriggling about," she instructed, trying her best to sound calm.

"Now just let your body float up. Puff up your belly. See? You rises to the top." Instantly, Villienne seemed to float much better.

"Hold fast," she burbled, trying not to take in water herself as she pushed Villienne to the surface and threaded her arm under his left armpit, clasping his right shoulder firmly.

Would wonders never cease! Little Jane marvelled. Her father *had* told her the truth. (Well, about the carry at least, the verdict was still out on the magic orange pips). Due to the increased buoyancy of the human body in water in comparison to air, Little Jane could carry Villienne in a way she never could have on land. By kicking her legs and swimming with her free arm, Little Jane could pull him along.

As light as the weedy magistrate was, and despite the increased buoyancy of salt water, after several minutes his weight became too heavy for Little Jane. Gradually, stroke by stroke, they were starting to sink and more of the briny water was finding its way into Little Jane's mouth. She felt like retching.

Villienne was horribly ashamed of being carried along in such an undignified manner, but it seemed there was no alternative. He desperately tried to will the land closer. Yet despite his plea, they didn't seem to be getting any nearer to shore. In fact, they were barely maintaining their position as the current worked against their tired bodies, pushing them sideways, parallel with the shore. Silently, he cursed himself for ever having claimed he could swim. What in the world had possessed him? Perhaps, in that most secret corner of his self, he'd grown tired of writing about heroes and longed, if only for a one stupid, mistaken moment to actually *be* one.

Heroic aspiration aside, he now saw that if he continued to cling to Little Jane, he would end up dragging them both down to a watery grave.

"Jane," he gasped when he saw her dark head surface. "You have to let me go. We'll both sink if you keep this up."

She paid him no mind and kept swimming.

It was hopeless. He turned away from the mighty volcanic mountain, ready to struggle free one last time, to sink himself on purpose and let her go on without him. It was then that he saw a very odd thing.

About a hundred yards away from where they struggled he saw a man — a man who appeared to be walking on water.

Villienne blinked, wondering if in his frenzied state he was hallucinating, but no, there was a man, a hearty, bare-chested fellow in breeches, strolling along as cheerfully as you please right on top of the waves. He wore a pair of spectacles that flashed in the sunlight, and now, as Villienne watched in amazement, he took them off to clean the lenses.

"Halloo there!" shouted Villienne. He waved his arms and splashed about in the water.

"What're you doing?" spluttered Little Jane as the magistrate slipped straight through her arms.

Looking over Villienne's head, she too was shocked by the strange vision of a shirtless man apparently hovering an inch above the sea.

"Hellooo!" shouted the Man-Who-Walked-on-Water.

As they got closer, Little Jane realized the man was actually standing on a rocky ledge in the water. But who was this man? Was he friend or foe?

"Villienne?" She turned, but he seemed to have slipped under the water again. Down she plunged after him.

As she pulled the soggy magistrate to the surface, he clawed the air like a man trying to climb an invisible ladder, his head still underwater. Together they struggled forward through the water, toward the man floating above them like a mirage.

Finally, Villienne bumped heavily into the rock wall. The man on the ledge helped as best he could as Villienne pulled himself up and onto it, thankful for its precious solidity.

Still coughing from all the water he'd swallowed, Villienne rolled over and sat up. Little Jane tried to pull herself out of the moat and onto the ledge beside him, but her numbed fingers couldn't seem to find purchase on the slippery rock. Villienne watched as the Man-Who-Walked-on-Water leaned forward, locked his hands under Jane's armpits, and pulled her up and out of the water. Little Jane let out a gasp as she flopped onto the slimy path like a fish pulled onto dry land.

She immediately began to cough, and the man crouched down and patted her gently on the back. Suddenly, Little Jane let out a loud burp and expelled a large amount of water in what Charity and Felicity would surely have condemned as an extremely unladylike gesture.

"Excuse her," said Villienne, eager to preserve a veneer of politeness before the stranger who'd saved them.

"Ha! The Nameless Isle. What a place," Little Jane said as she stretched out her arms to embrace the blue sky.

"Here, have a drink," offered the Man-Who-Walked-on-Water. He held out a canteen to her.

Little Jane took the container and proceeded to gulp down a large quantity of the water before passing it to Villienne. "Thankee, sir," she said to the man, wiping her mouth on the back of her hand.

Villienne drank the rest and turned to thank the man, but as he got a better look at their rescuer, his eyes nearly popped out of his head.

He opened his mouth, but what came out was unintelligible.

"Steady on. There's a good fellow," said the man calmly. "Now tell me, what's the trouble?"

"It c-c-can't b-b-be," Villienne stuttered.

"Uh, your pardon, young sir," the stranger said, turning to Little Jane. "But there appears to be something amiss with your companion. Is he sun-touched? Come, you can tell me. I'm a doctor."

"Lewy, it's me!" shouted Villienne, and he leapt to his feet to embrace the stranger.

"Wait. How do you know my name?"

"Oh, by Arbuthnot's epistle," groaned Villienne. "It's me, Lewiston."

"No, you're not Lewiston, *I'm* Lewiston," said the man. "Wait. Goodness, you're —"

"Villienne!" shouted Villienne.

"My college roommate!" exclaimed Lewiston in disbelief.

"A little moist, to be sure, but Sir Almost-Doctor Alistair Florence Virgil Villienne, all the same," proclaimed the magistrate.

"As I live and breathe. Villy? It is you!" cried the astonished doctor. "You grew a moustache."

"Yes," crowed Villienne, beaming proudly. "Yes, I did."

"But this is beyond belief. Fantastic. Stupendous."

"Sublime," added Villienne, laughing.

"Why, you sly fox. I knew someday our paths would cross again. Oh, I could tell there was greatness in this fellow," Lewiston said to Little Jane. "Dear, dear Alistair. I knew you would do something wonderfully unorthodox with yourself. And lo and behold, here you are. But goodness, you're soaked through. Did that frightful creature assault you as well?"

"What creature?" asked Little Jane, but the doctor was busy questioning Villienne.

"What are you doing here? Have you seen my captain? How did you find me? Do you think I'm much stouter than when you saw me last? What's the word on those peculiar orange birds? Degenerate flamingos or something more sinister? Oh, forget all that." Lewiston stopped himself at last and held his old friend at arm's length. "Of all the awful, lonely places on earth to find a friend." His eyes grew moist. "Come here." He clasped Villienne in a clammy hug, holding the stunned magistrate as Little Jane looked on with growing impatience.

"Villienne," Little Jane tugged on the magistrate's jacket. "What're you doing? We've no time for this. We need to —"

"You need to what?" Lewiston bent down to peer at Little Jane. "Who are you, little fellow?"

"I'm not a little fellow," growled Little Jane, hands on her hips. "Me name's Little Jane — no, Jane Silver," she corrected herself. "And who're you t'be asking?"

"My pardon for not introducing him sooner," Villienne said. "Little Jane, this is the esteemed Dr. Samuel Lewiston, one of the founding members of the Edinburgh College Amateur Dramatic Society and a close friend from my university years."

Doc Lewiston favoured Little Jane with a deep bow. "We were medical students together," he explained, "and until Alistair here accidentally incinerated our lodgings, flatmates as well."

Villienne blushed. "You know I still feel awful about that."

"All forgiven," the cheerful doctor assured him. "Now tell me, Villy, who is your young companion who most vociferously insists on *not* being a fellow. And what are you doing in literally the last place on earth I expected to find you?"

"We're looking for me parents," piped up Little Jane, eager to get back to the search.

"Your parents?" inquired Doc Lewiston, who only then began to realize there was something strangely familiar about the girl's appearance. "And just who might they be, eh? What did you say your last name was?"

"Silver," said Little Jane, a glint in her eye.

"Is that right?"

It was at that moment that Little Jane noticed that the path of rock they were standing on ran from the place they found the lamp, east to the volcanic mountain on the other shore. At high tide the water hid the path from sight, but now, as the tide was going out, the rocky strip stood revealed to all, rising a few inches up above the water. This path then, *this* was what Melvin's code had been trying to tell her about all this time, she realized.

"Masthead East *Lamp*!" she cried triumphantly as she pulled Melvin from his scabbard, holding up his handle for Villienne to see. "I *was* right! That lamp— it were supposed to lead the way!"

Chapter Fourteen

The Shiv

"Caw!" a peculiar orange bird screamed as its beady eyes peered down at the two ungainly figures struggling along the rocky path.

"Oh, do shut up," muttered Bonnie Mary at the irritating fowl, but this only seemed to further encourage the creature.

Beside her, Long John forced himself to take another painful hop forward, well aware he was leaning more heavily on Bonnie Mary with each step. His face was red with sunburn and sweat dripped into his eyes.

The treasure cave was still far off. It would take time for them to make their way around the base of the volcano to the right spot. Then they'd have to face the climb up the tightly twisting paths between the rocks, up to the cave that served as their own personal bank vault.

Suddenly, Bonnie Mary stopped, cocking her crown

of matted braids in the direction they'd come from. She listened intently, drops of perspiration glittering on her brow.

"What?" Long John asked. "What is it?"

"What's that?" she rasped, her throat dry.

"What? I don't hear …" And then he did. "Cannon fire? Could it be…? You think someone's come to rescue us?"

"Maybe it's not a rescue at all," said Bonnie Mary. "Could always be some other fella Fetz made angry come ta take it outta his hide. Sides, if it was Jonesy, Ishiro, or Little Jane, how'd they know where to find us?"

"They all three know that there's treasure on the island. And Jonesy knows exactly where the treasure's hid, and so does Jane, right? You gave her the sword."

"Aye, I did," replied Bonnie Mary. "Not that I been counting on Jonesy to remember much. It were so long ago, and you know how he be about remembering things. I should've reminded him now and again all these years. Still, maybe he did remember. Stranger things have happened, eh?" She took another halting step forward, half-dragging Long John along before another, much less pleasant thought occurred to her. "Wait. Jim, you did explain to Little Jane the meaning of the clues on the sword like you said you would, didn't you?

"Me?"

"Yes, you Jim!"

"Weren't it you what told her?" he asked hopefully.

"No."

"Blast it! I thought you'd tell her when you gave her the sword …"

"All my days. You'd think with all them stories yer always tellin' her, you'd tell her something she might actually be *needing* to know."

"Now, that ain't fair, Mary. You was the one gave her that sword. Weren't it only natural I assume it would be *you* what'd tell her? And warn't it your brilliant idea to stash the blasted loot here in the first place, now that I recollect it? I were always saying secret codes and hiding places ain't nothing but trouble, but you had to get inventive …"

"Oh, hush! It don't matter now. Our goose is *well* cooked and you know it, Jim Silver. If'n I ever get me hands on that dirty pox-monger Fetz, I swear I'll tear 'im in two."

Unfortunately, there was nothing they could do now other than curse themselves for being so negligent. Once more they were forced to hold fast and trudge on, in the desperate hope the cave would provide their timely salvation.

Madsea listened to the pounding of the far-off cannons with growing irritation. It was impossible, but somehow, someway, someone was here. On *his* island.

He'd been followed, betrayed. Someone had been tipped off, and now they were coming … *strangers* … after his gold. The gold he'd suffered and near died for, and curse them, but they were firing on the *Panacea* now, and she was firing back, albeit sporadically. He'd recognize the report of her 24-pounders anywhere.

He looked back and saw Kingly make it to shore and help Darsa out of the water and up onto the beach. The steward coughed up a copious amount of water as

Kingly gently pried his fingers off the scrap of wood he still clutched to his chest. Madsea felt a startling twinge of guilt when he noticed the absence of Doc Lewiston from the group of survivors. He'd long assumed the one benefit of prison was that it had beaten such useless sentiments out of him for good. That he harboured such unexpected sympathy for a doctor, of all people — a man who'd tried to put leeches on him, for Pete's sake — seemed beyond belief! Yet of all the people Madsea had met since his imprisonment by the French all those years ago, Lewiston was the first to show him any scrap of true kindness. That Lewiston stayed on to tend to him despite lucrative offers from other ships struck him as inexplicable, yet there it was.

"Ahoy, Cap'n," Kingly called out.

"Have you seen Lewiston?" asked Madsea, eager for some good news about the doctor.

"Sorry, Captain, looks like that creature got 'im."

Madsea sighed and turned away so the men could not see how upset he was. "How's Darsa faring?"

"A'right, Captain," choked out Darsa. "Just need a moment to catch me breath."

"It sounds like someone's attacking the *Panacea*, Cap'n" announced Kingly gravely.

"Ship'll have to take care of herself," Madsea replied, unfazed. "There's no way for us to get back at the moment. The only prudent course to salvage anything of our mission is to press on and get to that treasure afore anyone else has a chance to lay hands on it. That's where our priority lies!"

"Yes, sir," replied Kingly, though he felt there might be something slightly amiss with the captain's reasoning. However, his position was not to ask questions. He helped Darsa sit up against a rock to recover.

When Kingly looked up from tending to his friend, he saw that Madsea was already running toward what appeared to be a path that led up the side of the mountain. He watched, amazed at his captain's healthy pace. Instead of slackening, Madsea seemed to pick up speed as he went, his boots pounding across the sand in time to the distant sound of the cannons.

Bonnie Mary glanced over her shoulder, dismayed to spy Madsea gaining on them, loping over the flat tops of the beach rocks like a man who'd never been sick a day in his life. He still carried Jim's crutch over his shoulder like a club, and looked as if he meant to use it.

"Sod it," panted Long John, "Did I miss something here, or ain't he a bleeding half-dead consumptive?"

"Don't look back, Jim, just keep going," puffed Bonnie Mary as she pulled him by the scraps of shirt tied about his waist. They would have to quit soon, a distant part of her mind realized; Jim couldn't endure much more.

"Mary, stop!" he finally gasped.

Stubbornly she continued to pull him along.

"No," he croaked out and abruptly let go of her.

"Jim, we can't stop here!" Tears stung her eyes. "Fetz, he be catching up …"

"No," Jim repeated weakly, leaning his weary bulk against a massive black rock to rest, his chest heaving. "Where's the shiv?"

"What?"

"Me knife, Mary. Where it be?"

"What for, Jim?"

"You'll get on ahead faster without me," he panted.

"Jim, I ain't leaving you here. Fetz'll kill you."

"No, he won't. You just get on up there and open the chest lickety-split. Get whatever weapons you finds, then come back for me. Whatever new health Fetz's come into, I'm still a mite stronger 'n him, I figure. With the shiv I'll take him easy, you'll see."

He favoured her with his most winning smile. Though his lips were split and flecked with blood, that smile still could not help but bend her stubborn heart. She could stay here to wait for Fetz to come, but she knew Jim was right about the weapons in the cave. The only way the two of them could hold out against Fetz and his men was with the weapons. And it was plain to see that Jim would never make it up to the cave, even with her help. Still, Bonnie Mary couldn't leave him. Never had she seen Jim so hurt and beaten down. Even now, supporting himself against a rock, he seemed to weave to and fro in the air, barely able to hold himself upright. He didn't look strong enough take on even the tubercular Madsea, let alone any of the strong sailors who might accompany their captain.

"C'mon Mary." He nudged her. "There be no other way."

"I reckon. But still …" She took a deep breath. Her damaged eye cried freely and Jim reached up a trembling hand to brush the wetness away. Even that small movement, she saw, seemed to take extraordinary effort.

"Keep yer wits about ya, Jim," she whispered, not trusting herself to say more. Her gaze darted quickly over his features, trying to memorize them all, every pore and crease of that face she loved and so feared to lose.

Oh Lord, forgive me, she thought. With a sharp gasp, she burst the bodice of her dress, tearing it in half with her tough, strong hands, releasing the shiv knife inside at last. She picked it up and held it out.

"Take it, Jim!"

He reached out and took the shiv from her. Their eyes met. *How can I leave him?* she thought.

"Get on!" he said roughly, pushing her away, breaking the spell.

"You stay safe, Jim," she whispered, her voice choked with emotion. "Captain's orders, ye hear."

"Aye aye," he replied.

She turned and ran off up the path and out of sight.

As soon as she was gone he sagged heavily against the rock. *I be dying here, most like,* he thought, and yet he felt strangely calm. He was too tired for fear. The thought that Bonnie Mary might escape comforted him. He closed his eyes and prayed that she would be safe.

Then, with a few jarring hops, he propelled himself behind a massive black boulder on the side of the path. From there he knew he would be hidden from view of anyone coming up the path. The world swam before his eyes for a moment, and he felt the urge to lie down on the soft, welcoming sand. But there he remained, crouched and leaning against the rock, hidden from view, the shiv in his hand, waiting.

As Madsea scrambled up the path he felt a strange sense of agility he had not possessed since the days of his early youth as a cabin boy aboard the *Pieces of Eight*. Had he been less interested in treasure and the demise of his enemies that day, he might have taken a bit of time to wonder why this was so. The mind of Madsea, however, remained inflexibly bent toward the attainment of his goal and all he realized was that his strength, renewed as it was, was still not enough. Years of damage to his lungs could not be reversed so quickly. As he made his way around the mountain, he began to grow short of breath, with the pirates still far ahead of him.

Once Darsa appeared to be out of danger, Kingly left the beach and quickly caught up with his captain. Spotting the distant figure of Bonnie Mary high above them on the path, Kingly surged forward, overtaking his captain. Unbeknownst to him, the poor bosun was set on a direct course past a certain black boulder that hid far more than a stray patch of lichen.

Long John knew he would only have one chance to overpower Fetz. In his mind he saw himself leaping out from behind the rock, shiv knife in hand, and landing on Madsea's back just as the *Panacea*'s captain came up the path. From there, Long John figured he could slip the knife in between Madsea's ribs, thrusting upward to the fatal place using his greater weight and momentum to force his smaller, lighter enemy down beneath him. He could pin Madsea to the ground then, stabbing him once more, should the first thrust not meet its intended mark. He forced himself to breath more slowly. Whatever the outcome, it would all be over soon.

Now Long John heard the sound of running feet upon the path, every footfall beating in his head like a drum. It took all his will power to keep from springing out too soon. *Wait … wait … wait …*

Now!

He sprang.

In the millisecond between his leap from behind the rock and the time it took for his body to fall on the man on the path below, Long John realized he'd made a terrible error. This man was too large to be Madsea. But he had no time to adjust his thrust in mid-air, and he landed on the big body with the sharp point of his blade exposed. The shiv struck flesh and bone somewhere in the man's side as he twisted. Long John could not shove the blade home for the final deadly push now. How could he, when he had no idea whom he'd just stabbed? All he knew was that the man could not possibly be his intended target.

Kingly bucked wildly under his attacker's weight. A geyser of blood sprayed up as Long John held on to the large man's shoulders, still dangling a few feet off the ground, slippery hands trying to find purchase on the knife to pull it out, should he need it to defend himself.

Just then, Long John heard a cry from somewhere behind him. Still riding the thrashing Kingly's back, he turned toward the sound. A large object was coming straight for him. He had time to partially duck his head away from the swing, but the club still connected with his skull. Pain and bright lights exploded in his head as his hands released their grip. Slipping off the bosun, Long John hit the ground, already unconscious.

Madsea watched as Jim fell to the dust at his feet. Faint from his wound and loss of blood, Kingly collapsed beside the senseless pirate.

Madsea stood panting over the two men, the wooden crutch still vibrating in his hands from the force of the hit. Dizziness and a faintly floating feeling came over him. Had he done it? Had he finally dealt the fatal blow? But the treasure. How would he ever find it now?

Somewhere, far away, Madsea heard a hastily cut off scream. His strength returned as he remembered Bonnie Mary. Madsea peered up at the string of holes that pockmarked the side of the mountain. The treasure must be hidden in one of those caves. And she would lead him right to it. As he scanned the mountainside, he glimpsed a movement. Just below the place where the mountain's surface abruptly turned into sheer black rock, he saw her, a brightly coloured parrot in her garish clothes, standing out clearly against the sombre black of the volcanic stone.

A joyful smile, like that of a little boy, bloomed on Madsea's sunken face. He picked his way around the bodies of Long John and Kingly, not stopping to check if either still held a pulse. Eager to be on his way, he climbed in the direction of Bonnie Mary, up, up toward the caves.

Bonnie Mary ran between two boulders, cursing as she scraped her knuckles on a piece of jutting rock.

Jim!

Don't think, just run. Don't think, just run.

Please be all right, Jim. Please be all right.

These desperate thoughts broke through all efforts to calm herself.

Damn her eyes and the twisting path, but she couldn't see anything of the fight from where she stood, listening. There'd been shouted curses and screams of pain. Those she heard.

It took all her willpower to keep from turning back. She had to keep her head, save the emotion for later. Her only job now was to get to the cave and get the weapons before Madsea or any of his men. Then she could help Jim. Not now.

She took off again, rounding a bend, following the corkscrew path around the mountain. She passed by the cool gaping mouths of several welcoming caves along the way. Her lungs gasped for air and she was sorely tempted to stop and take shelter in one, but knew it was a foolish idea. Now that her knife was gone, she needed something to arm herself with. If Madsea dared survive, she would not meet him with fists alone.

Madsea settled into a brisk walk. There was no point in running. Bonnie Mary could run all she liked, he thought with a grim smile, but ultimately there was no place for her to go. He was fairly certain this was the only path up the mountain.

Above a small clump of stunted pear trees — the only trees that grew anywhere on the island, it seemed — sat a small statue. Once the statue had been painted gold, but now only a scattering of paint flakes hinted at its former glory. At one time, long ago, the golden, eight-armed figure looked as if it had swallowed the mighty sun itself. The statue and the clump of trees with their hard yellow pears were all that distinguished this particular cave from the hundreds of others dotting the volcanic mountain.

Bonnie Mary looked down at the ebbing tide far below; low enough now to expose the bridge of raised rock that ran from the bottom-most pear tree away to the other side of the moat, the path she'd taken on every journey to the treasure cave — except this one. Three dark specks moved along the tide-exposed path in the distance, but she could not say who or even *what* they were.

With a final bound over the rocks at the mouth of the cave, Bonnie Mary launched herself into its blessed shade, hoping, just this once, that chance would favour her.

Chapter Fifteen

The Treasure Cave

Jonesy crept along the black sand, watching the last of the sailors disappear over the black rocks. Now he planned to make his way back to wait for Little Jane and the magistrate.

He checked the pistol for shot and powder, but discovered the entire mechanism was soaked and useless. At least the heavy weapon might prove useful to conk someone over the head with if it came to that.

Suddenly, Jonesy heard a noise. He looked up and saw a figure sliding out of control down the slope of rock right above him. Before Jonesy could react, the man fell in a shower of stones at his feet.

Jonesy, for all his supposed cloudy-headedness, had the newcomer pegged in an instant. As the large man stood up and began brushing off the stony debris, Jonesy moved forward and jammed the barrel of the recently-acquired pistol against his neck. "Well, if it ain't me old china, Ned Ronk."

"Let me go," whimpered Ned. His startled eyes moved over Jonesy's face before coming to rest on the familiar prison brand on his shoulder. "Come on, ain't I always been a decent customer down the pub?"

"Hmmmm," mused Jonesy, "frequent customer, more like. Hardly decent. Decent don't hold me baby cousin over the side of a deck rail."

"It's Captain Madsea you be wantin', Jonesy, not me," protested Ned, hands raised. "They weren't my ideas, none of them things what I did."

"Maybe this Captain Madsea told you t'do them things and maybe he didn't," answered the barkeep amiably, still making no move to attack. "Don't really matter now, do it? Much as it'd give me pleasure to see him go down, he ain't here. So, I'll just have to satisfy meself with knocking your loaf off instead, inn'it?"

"Leave off," begged Ned. "I ain't the one what give the orders. I never harmed yer precious Jane, not really."

"And how'd you reckon whether you done her harm or no? Don't matter who gave you the order. You was well chuffed to do it. You think I ain't been around? You think you're such an uncommon man? Pah! I knows you for what you are, Ned Ronk. Knowed men like you aplenty back in London. Still, we took you in, gave you a second chance, made you part of us. And in exchange you betrays us."

"Please, Jonesy. I didn't mean it."

A deep furrow creased Jonesy's brow. "Oh, I think you're done, bruv. You're done."

With his last chance to weasel out of his predicament evaporating before his eyes, Ned panicked. He struck out at Jonesy with a frantic lunge forward. Jonesy swatted him away as if he were nothing more than a large island mosquito. With a sharp crack, the grip of Jonesy's pistol connected with the former bosun's nose, but one hit wasn't enough to take down a man as large as Ned Ronk. Jonesy, despite his bulk, was the older man and longer out of practice. His movements were slower than he remembered, Ned Ronk's quicker than he expected.

"Mr. Jones," Ned taunted Jonesy, defiantly wiping at the stream of blood gushing from his nostrils. "Somethin' wrong with yer pistol?"

"No!"

"Then why ain't ye used it yet?"

"Maybe something's wrong with me pistol," growled Jonesy, "or maybe I think you ain't worth the shot."

"Ha!" spat Ned. And with that, he hurled himself at Jonesy, fists at the ready. Jonesy leapt back in time and Ned only managed to land a punch on the barkeep's beefy upper arm, where it barely hurt him at all. Ned's body continued to move forward from the force of his punch, and Jonesy took the opportunity to hit the back of his head with handle of the pistol as hard as he could.

Ned hit the ground, out cold.

"Like I said, not worth the shot," repeated Jonesy as he stood over Ned's motionless form. Still breathing hard from the unaccustomed exertion, he carefully rolled his foe over. Ned remained unconscious, but breathing steadily.

"Now all we needs is something to tie you up with," said Mr. Jones.

In the cool confines of the cave, Bonnie Mary stopped to catch her breath and allow her vision to adjust to the gloom before venturing farther in. About twenty paces from the mouth of the cave she saw them, dozens and dozens of chests of varying shapes and sizes, from the most delicately carved ivory jewel box to wood crates large enough for a man to sit in.

She scanned the boxes until she spotted one decorated with carvings of elephants. This particular chest they'd taken off a British merchantman south of Calcutta a few years back. Though it'd been a while since she'd seen the ivory-handled dagger it contained, she still remembered the damage its previous owner had caused with it. If only it would work so well for her.

None of the chests were ever locked, the remote location of the treasure cache considered protection enough against thieves. The rusty clasp of the elephant box proved resistant, but after some prying the lid of the chest finally opened with a loud complaining creak.

At last!

Bonnie Mary stared into the chest, stunned. She blinked, as if to clear her vision of the implausible sight. *Where was that tell-tale glimmer of precious stone? That happy shimmer of silver and gold?*

She rubbed her eyes and looked again.

Impossible!

She raised the chest over her head and shook it, but the only thing inside the chest was … well, the inside of a chest! And even that wasn't fully there, she realized with escalating panic. There was a gaping hole in the back of the chest, as if something had eaten straight through the wood. Rats? Termites?

Bonnie Mary tossed the chest aside. There were other weapons in other boxes — jewelled daggers, silver pistols. She picked up a large, heavy-looking box. She nearly fell backward, the chest was so much lighter than it should have been. With a feeling of ominous dread, she yanked off the lid.

Of course it was light, light as air; for air was all it contained.

Desperation setting in, she tossed the box away and pulled the rusty latch up on a third. This chest, too, was empty.

With short, panicked breaths she grasped at another. And another.

Empty. Empty.

All empty!

Bonnie Mary could not understand it. It couldn't be real. It couldn't be true. Her mind churned with questions.

To take all the treasure in one go was physically impossible without a large crew of people. It'd taken her and Jim years to accumulate all the chests in the cave, carrying only a few between them every year. Some of the chests were even older than that and had been put there for safekeeping by old Thomas Bright, long ago. Why would someone take all the treasure without the chests to carry it in? It just didn't make sense. They'd last been on the island only a few months before. The treasure had all been there then, hadn't it? When was the last time she and Jim had checked inside any of the chests?

Bonnie Mary thought back, trying to remember. Was it five years ago? Ten?

But it all had to be there — a haul like that didn't just vanish. And yet it was gone, all gone.

How to explain it? Theft? Ludicrous! How could a pirate *get* any safer than a cursed island with no name, never committed to any naval chart with no known inhabitants? Bonnie Mary glanced furtively around the shadowy cavern, checking for signs of any foreign presence. Nothing. No new marks in the grey-black dust, apart from the usual orange bird tracks. All was as it had always been, no different from when she and Jim last left the cave.

Not a thing was out of place, and yet there were holes in the chests and the gold and weapons were gone. It was too much for her weary mind to comprehend. The realization of it whirled around her like the confounding winds of a hurricane.

A sudden noise outside the cave made her jump. In her shock over the missing treasure, she'd momentarily forgotten the men pursuing her and the fight down below, the outcome of which remained a mystery. She tensed as she listened to the echoing sound of footsteps on the rocks outside the cave. The sound of her pursuer's even gait only confirmed what she already suspected — it was her enemy, Fetz, coming up the path now, her sweet Jim lost to her forever.

Her hands curled into fists at her sides as she sniffed back her tears. *Nothing for it!* She cast her gaze desperately over the chests for a weapon, any weapon she could use against him. With grim determination she picked up the elephant box. *You don't need the dagger*, she thought. *You don't need no more than this. His blood for what he done to Jim!*

She raised the chest above her head just as a dark silhouette appeared in the mouth of the cave.

As she suspected, it was the scarecrow-thin shape of Fetzcaro Madsea.

In a red haze of fury, Bonnie Mary hurled the chest at his head, but Madsea sidestepped her throw, suffering only a glancing blow. The box crashed to the ground behind him and bounced over the edge of the cliff, smashing to pieces on the rocks below.

Somewhere far away, a peculiar orange bird screamed, echoing her rage and frustration.

Cautiously, Madsea entered the cave, the crutch slung over his shoulder.

Bonnie Mary grabbed another empty treasure chest and held it out as both a shield and a weapon. "Halt!" she cried in warning, as she stepped back into the darker recesses of the cave.

Somewhere close by, Madsea heard the eerie, echoing cries of the Nameless Isle's peculiar orange fowl. From under the shadow of the box, Bonnie Mary's good eye flashed malevolently back up at him. He shivered involuntarily, but then his expression softened.

Gently, like an animal tamer coaxing a savage tiger from its den, he whispered, "Please, Mary. I won't hurt you."

She was weeping now, he could see, tears marking clean tracks down her dusty cheeks and he was sure he could turn her weak, feminine feelings to his advantage if he just used the right words.

"You was just a girl when Jim betrayed me," he said softly. "You were wounded. It wasn't your ..." The next part proved exceedingly difficult for him to say, even in such circumstances. "It wasn't your *fault*. Not your fault at all. I know that now. I'm not a man without reason." He attempted a smile. "Now it falls to you to use *your* reason and do what's fitting. No more tricks. Just show me the treasure and I'll let you go, you have me word."

He stuck out a long-fingered hand, but she made no move to lower the chest, though her arms ached from holding it aloft.

"Show me your cache of gold and I'll let you go," Madsea repeated. "You can leave here free as a bird. Free to find your daughter. Think of that. All you must do is show me. Be sensible. There's nothing to be gained from this. Surely, you see that."

He paused, giving her time to consider.

But his generous offer of clemency was only met with an explosion of bitter laughter. "Oh, Fetz, you're such a fool."

A cannon boomed somewhere in the distance.

"Can't you see you're beat? You and me both. Chance take us all, we're done. There's nothing here. Nothing for me and nothing for you, so by all means let's share." She laughed shakily.

"Silence, woman!" Madsea barked, raising the crutch again. "What're you babbling about?"

She brushed her sleeve across one eye, then the other. He wasn't sure whether she was laughing or crying or both. "If I ain't knowed better, I'd say your ship's under fire."

"I know about me ship!" he shouted. "Now where's the bleedin' treasure?"

She shrugged. "See for yourself."

He glanced at the open chests scattered around her. They were all empty. It made no sense. Could Jim and Mary truly plan that far ahead? Who was here to do their bidding with them in the brig of the *Panacea* the whole time?

Madsea shook his head. "Enough tricks, woman! Open the rest of the boxes." Under his watchful eyes she began opening the remaining chests. One by one, Bonnie Mary lifted each lid. One by one they found each as empty inside as the last. All had the same holes at the back as that first chest. What obscure instrument was used to make the holes and what manner of man had wielded it remained a mystery.

After nearly half an hour of prying open rusty clasps they were down to the last chest in the cavern, but still they'd found no treasure.

Madsea refused to accept what his eyes plainly told him. *It had to be a trick. Just another one of Jim's tricks.*

In a sudden motion he crossed the space between them and seized Bonnie Mary by her shirt. He shook her like an oversized doll, the cowry shells woven into her braids clacking noisily together.

"What've you done with it all, wench?"

"Why won't you believe me? It's gone, and I gots just as much idea of where to as you do," she spat back at him.

The wheels of thought were beginning to turn again in Bonnie Mary's mind. Madsea would not remain shocked by the treasure's disappearance for long, she knew. And without the treasure, there would be nothing preventing him from destroying her and Jim. Assuming, that is, that Jim wasn't already—

No! She gulped. The only thing to do was buy some time.

"Poof! Just up and vanished. What do you take me for?" Madsea asked angrily.

"You might be rather put out if I told you," she retorted.

"Open that last one. I'm on to you now. The rest are decoys, aren't they? The whole lot's concentrated in that last one, inn'it?"

But when Bonnie Mary pried the final chest open, it was identical inside to all the others; empty, with the same strange holes bored into the back.

"But there must be more," muttered Madsea desperately. "There must be." He crouched down to peer into the shadows of the cave. "I saw something over here. What's that?"

Bonnie Mary took this brief lapse in his attention to heft up the chest she had just opened. In one strong, unbroken motion she swung it at Madsea's head. But the pirate hunter saw the movement out of the tail of his eye, and just in time he managed to parry the chest with his club. The strength of the meeting between the two sent the timber of the crutch to shivering in Madsea's hand. As the violence of the contact ran up his arm, the wooden instrument split in two and Madsea fell to the ground.

With her enemy distracted, Bonnie Mary tried to make a break for it. She lunged toward the mouth of the cave, but once again Madsea was too fast for her. He grabbed her ankle with his hand, bringing her down, hard. He stood on top of her now, panting, the adrenaline coursing through his starved system, one foot planted securely on her chest. He dug the heel of his climbing boot into her and Bonnie Mary cringed as she felt his cleats pierce through the material of her shirt. Still, she managed to spit out what they both could plainly see: "Fetz, whatever you be wanting to believe, there's no conspiracy here — me and Jim's got nothing to do with this. It's just gone."

She was truly frightened now, for she knew there would be nothing to stop Fetz from destroying her right there in his anger. Not to mention that whatever force had violated the chests was still out there, lurking somewhere. It was just a matter of waiting for the blow, whichever party it came from first. "Just accept it." She sighed helplessly. "It's gone."

"No." Fetzcaro was suddenly calm. A benign, almost placid smile spread strangely over his hollow features. "No, it's *not*." His gaze had moved from Bonnie Mary and he was now staring at something at the back of the cave. Something had caught his eye.

Straining, Bonnie Mary finally saw what he was looking at — a single gold sovereign lying on the floor, glittering in the dim light.

"Look!" Madsea shouted gleefully. "There's more!"

He glanced down at Bonnie Mary, still lying under his boot, then back across the cavern. More pieces lay glittering there, a trail of bright gold against the black rock, winking seductively at him from the shadows. To go after the gold he would need to release her.

"Here," he said, pulling her roughly to her feet. "You walk ahead. I know that treasure's still here. Don't think I won't figure out what you done with it."

Grateful for this sudden reprieve, Bonnie Mary stood and brushed herself off.

Madsea pushed her ahead. "*Move.* No tricks."

Together they followed the little trail of coins that led to the back wall of the cave, Madsea picking them up to line his pockets with as they went along.

"That's it," Bonnie Mary said flatly as they reached the back wall of the cave. "There's nowhere else to go."

Except, much to Bonnie Mary's astonishment, she saw that there *was*. The interior of the cave did not end in a flat back wall as she and Jim had long supposed. Instead, the floor slanted down. Madsea pushed her roughly ahead as the incline got steeper. As she walked farther, the walls began to narrow. Soon they found themselves in a tunnel, just wide enough for one person to pass through with ease. They proceeded in single file, with Bonnie Mary in front, feeling their way through the inky darkness, the walls close around them.

The air grew hot and stale as they descended. With Madsea's hand still pushing, Bonnie Mary forced herself to go on, knowing the weight of the mountain overhead could crush them at any moment. As the roof of the tunnel sank lower they had to walk with their heads bent, no longer able to stand erect. The air grew so stale she felt like she couldn't breathe, the darkness around them more complete than any night she'd ever seen. And still, Madsea pushed her onward, deeper, into the bowels of the mountain.

Occasionally, Bonnie Mary would hear the echoing call of a bird as she felt her way through the blackness. Oddly, the birds' cries seemed much closer now, though she knew that was impossible. She wondered if she was beginning to lose her mind from the terrible pressure of the mountain above her.

She crawled on with her eyes closed. Closed or open, it made no difference, all was dark.

She prayed desperately. *Dear Lord, please don't let me die here, caught in a tunnel of rock, so close and cramped about me. Don't bury me in this great black mountain. Me, who's lived me whole life like the wind on a wave. Just let me see the green water and blue sky again, Lord. Oh, don't let me end here. No, no, no, not here.*

If Fetz prayed now or thought anything at all, Bonnie Mary couldn't tell. Did he hear the birds as well? Listening carefully, she could pick out a number of distinct bird calls now, some lower, some higher. At times a particular cry might even be answered by a chorus of others, until the whole tunnel rang with the echoing sounds. To her ears their warbling seemed almost human, like the quavering voices of aged crones, speaking some language all their own. Maybe they were the ghosts of dead sailors trapped here as she soon would be, warning doomed visitors of their fate.

Bonnie Mary shivered.

The ceiling of the tunnel finally became so low that they were forced to crawl along on their hands and knees. The air was growing steadily hotter, but no longer tasted so stale; instead it took on an oddly familiar odour that Bonnie Mary just couldn't place. And still the tunnel grew narrower. Just as she thought the hole would at last grow too small for them to go any farther, she saw a faint glow up ahead.

"Look!" she cried, nearly babbling with relief. "Daylight! The tunnel must come out on the other side of the mountain! That's why I heard the birds and —"

"Quiet," hissed Madsea. "Keep moving."

Whatever exit the birds had found, Bonnie Mary hoped it could accommodate a full-sized human.

Suddenly, the passageway widened abruptly and they could stand up again. There was a sudden rush of heat and the visible air unfurled itself around them, half lit by the weak reddish light up ahead.

Madsea found himself growing quite warm in the sudden humidity, his shirt and breeches clinging wetly to his body. The sulphurous smell in the air unexpectedly recalled to his mind a fashionable hot spring in Bath. In the reddish glow he watched the steamy swirls of vapour move around him like ghostly dancers.

Red steam? Bonnie Mary wondered, perplexed. Was the sun setting already? Had they truly been in the tunnel that long? And where was all this vapour coming from?

Before she could ponder these incongruities further, the passageway angled abruptly downward. With Madsea behind her and no way to back up, Bonnie Mary felt herself skidding down the incline, forced into a stumbling run.

As she slipped and slid, the tunnel opened wide before her. It was at this point that Madsea lost his footing and bowled into her, knocking her down. Together they tumbled down a smooth incline and emerged through a thick cloud of steam to find themselves suddenly landing on level ground.

Disentangling herself from Madsea, Bonnie Mary sat up and straightened her shirt. She noticed that the rock beneath her was a featureless black and strangely warm to the touch, yet stranger still was the bizarre sight that met her eyes when she chanced to look up.

It was as if someone had opened a Turkish bath-house in the centre of the mountain. Clouds of steam blanketed the ground. The air was intensely humid, but unlike the baths it was filled with the stench of sulphur and bird guano.

She clambered shakily to her feet, her good eye quickly adjusting to the dim light of the cavern. As the scene before her sharpened, her jaw dropped in surprise. A Turkish bath house would have made more sense than what she now saw before her.

She turned around, open-mouthed with disbelief.

Jim, if you could only see this!

At the moment, however, all Jim could see as he opened his bruised eyelids and blinked himself back into consciousness was the broad chest of Kingly. With a groan, he rolled himself off the bosun's body and sat up. Every part of his body vied painfully for his attention at the exact same moment. His head spun so badly he had to hold it in his hands.

Buck up, old man. You've had worse, he cajoled himself, but even *he* didn't buy that one. His skull hurt and his mouth hurt, and as he shifted clumsily in the black dust, his broken knee and bruised shoulder nearly blinded him with pain. The skin of his palms and the sole of his foot were scraped raw and bleeding, and his eyes were beginning to swell shut from the blow to his head. He was a mess, no question.

Yet as awful as this all was, what pained him most at the moment, what hurt him more than any ache in his ache-filled body, was the thought of Bonnie Mary caught in Madsea's clutches. It was that thought alone that forced him to crawl back and retrieve the knife from where it lay in the dust by the motionless bosun.

"Sorry, mate," he mumbled through split lips as he turned the bosun aside. "It weren't meant for you. I'll bury you decent, once this be over, I give you me word."

"Aye, aye, Cap'n," came the slurred reply from the body on the ground. Long John nearly dropped the shiv, he was so startled. The bosun moaned and grabbed at his side where the knife had cut his flank. Long John inched backward. There was no way of telling how badly Kingly was injured. He'd best be going before the big ox fully woke up.

With a Herculean effort he pulled himself up on a nearby boulder. Standing up again, he swayed unsteadily, the world blurring around him.

He realized in panic that he was going to fall, and that slight surge of terror gave him the tiny bit of energy he needed to remain upright and awake.

He thought of Bonnie Mary and dug his fingers into the rock, concentrating on its coolness, its utter solidity. He conjured her face before him and the dizziness passed. He dared to take a small hop forward and all the bones in his body seemed to jangle loose within him. It was a near thing, but he managed to stay upright.

Something was wrong, though. Ordinarily his balance was flawless, but now the ground seemed to be tilting this way and that like a deck in a storm. He tried another hop forward, but this time he tripped, staggered forward, and came crashing down painfully to the ground, mashing his nose against his arm. Blood leaked from his nose, but he was too tired to wipe it away.

What're ye lying here for? Move, ye useless lump. Get up n' save her, he thought angrily to himself. But try as he might, he just couldn't stand up. All he could do was move forward like a snail, trying to ignore the disturbing feel of something wet and sticky soaking through the knotted-off leg of his breeches. A cool breeze gently pushed his damp curls from his forehead. He swallowed and crawled forward, inching slowly to the rescue.

Chapter Sixteen

The Secret of the
Orange Birds

Doc Lewiston had barely begun his explanation of how he'd become acquainted with Little Jane's parents when Little Jane interrupted him.

"They're alive! They're alive!" she shouted, overjoyed with relief.

"Well, yes, at least they were the last time I saw them," he added, somewhat flustered.

"Then what're we waiting for? Let's go after 'em." With that, Little Jane bolted off along the path toward the mountain.

"Wait!" shouted Villienne.

He and Doc Lewiston looked at each other, shrugged, then took off after her, doing their best not to fall on the slippery surface.

The rock bridge ended in a short spit of grey-black sand on the other side. The enormous shadow of the volcanic mountain loomed over it, nearly blocking out the sun. The peak of the volcano was so high that it appeared to curve down toward them, bending to meet the horizon like a tall man lowering his head to enter a doorway.

Villienne leapt lightly onto a flat rock on the other side of the bridge and looked around. He spotted Little Jane a little ways ahead. She was already clambering up a narrow trail that wound its way between huge boulders at the base of the mountain. He craned his neck and could just make out what appeared to be dozens of caves dotting the side of the rock face above her.

He lost sight of her as she disappeared behind a large boulder. All of a sudden he heard a high-pitched scream from behind the rock. When Villienne and Lewiston got there, out of breathe, they found Little Jane standing in the middle of the path.

"I thought it was Papa," gasped Little Jane. The sand beneath her feet was speckled with blood. Little Jane stood over the body of a large man. "Is he … is he dead?" her voice twisted in fear.

Villienne looked away, blinking back tears himself, resisting the sick feeling that rose in his throat at the sight of the red liquid pooling around the body.

"Who is he?" asked Little Jane.

"The *Panacea*'s quartermaster, Kingly," answered Doc Lewiston as he approached the body. He mopped his sorrowful face with his handkerchief and bent down for a closer look. "Looks like he's been shot."

"Oh, for goodness sake, can't you get anything right?" complained the exasperated bosun, startling them all by abruptly sitting up. "I ain't been shot, I been stabbed. Then I knocked meself in the head when I fell. And I ain't the bleedin' quartermaster neither," he continued crossly. "I'm the bosun. You only been serving aboard ship for what, eight months? I mean, I knows you're just a surgeon, but *come on.*"

Doc Lewiston's eyes nearly popped straight out of his head at the bosun's apparent resurrection, but Little Jane didn't miss a beat.

She drew Melvin out and crouched down beside Kingly. "Where's me father and mother?" she asked. "Captains Bright and Silver, you know them? Tell us now or by thunder, I'll run ye through!"

"They's with the cap'n," replied Kingly, taken aback by the strange girl's intense demeanour.

"Where's the Captain?" asked Doc Lewiston, worriedly.

"Gone to get his treasure, I wager, without a thought to the likes o' us," Kingly said with an irritated wave. "And he can have it, ye ask me. Let 'im rot here with it for all I care!"

"Thanks for your help," said Villienne, turning to follow Little Jane, who had already started up the path. Lewiston made to follow.

"What about me then?" asked the injured bosun indignantly. "I near been stabbed cleaned through. All a' you just gonna up and leave me like this? What if I bleed to death? Don't nobody care about poor Kingly what never did a lick a harm to no one," sobbed the big man piteously.

Doc Lewiston stopped in his tracks. Much as he wanted to help his friends and save his captain, he could not in good conscience leave an injured man. Villienne may have been a dabbling almost-doctor, but Lewiston was a ship's surgeon in earnest and he'd sworn his oath to the *Panacea*'s crew.

"You two go on," he called to his companions before turning to his new patient.

"Don't worry, my good man, the cut doesn't appear too deep. First thing we get back to the ship, I'll get some nice fat leeches on you and you'll be right as rain, you'll see."

Satisfied to see Kingly left in more competent medical hands than his own, Villienne waved back at his long-lost friend, then sprinted after Little Jane, eager to be away from all the blood before he fell into a swoon.

"Through caverns measureless to man, down to a sunless sea,"* Madsea said in awe, stretching out a tremulous hand to touch the tendrils of curling yellow vapour rising from the ground. Unable to think of words of his own to describe the sight, he'd found himself speaking lines of long-forgotten poetry, as if fever-touched once more.

He and Bonnie Mary were in a hollow chamber inside the mountain that was high and wide enough to accommodate two tall ships side by side. Though there was no "sunless sea" in the centre of the cavern, there *were* several pools of strange glowing liquid. This was the source of the light they'd seen from the tunnel, Bonnie Mary realized. It was not the red light of the

---

* From the poem *Kubla Khan* by Samuel Taylor Coleridge.

distant setting sun, but the hot, red glow of something else — lava. The lava appeared to be mixed with something else. The edges of the pools were crusted with large yellow crystals of what looked like sulphur, which would account for the horrid smell in the cavern.

Peculiar orange birds congregated around these pools in astounding numbers, despite the heat. There must have been hundreds of them gathered there, more than Bonnie Mary had ever seen before. She saw flocks aplenty of the spindly-legged variety she was used to seeing on the island, their orange crested heads bobbing back and forth like metronomes. Then there were smaller, patchy-feathered birds, which she took to be the juveniles of the species. She even saw baby chicks with no feathers at all, their skin the colour of pale cantaloupe flesh, waddling about on bandy legs. The patchy juveniles made it their business to herd these chicks away from the dangerous lava pools, nipping and squeaking at them to keep them in line, looking for all the world like bossy older siblings.

As unusual as all this was, it was nothing compared to what Bonnie Mary saw when she looked up.

At first she thought the objects she saw were oddly shaped stalactites and stalagmites, natural formations of water droplets in caves over millennia. Yet the tall columns contained shapes and textures that just didn't seem right for something created by the process of nature alone. Had an ancient, long-deceased island tribe created them? Were they bizarre statues, perhaps, or tall symbolic thrones? The more she stared at the glittering columns, the more confident she felt that these were not formed naturally by the simple passage of time. Yet they were not things made by people either, she thought with a sudden jolt of comprehension, finally realizing what the objects were.

Nests! They were nests — fantastic golden nests! It seemed strange beyond belief, but it had to be true, for sitting atop each golden column, high up near the ceiling of the cavern, was a bird.

These were no ordinary birds, though. The golden nests were not the only things of abnormal size in the cavern. The orange birds that sat upon these marvellous creations were equally gigantic. To even call these peculiar birds "orange" seemed a grave injustice. Their luxuriant plumage ran the gamut of the entire orange spectrum, from pumpkin, jacinth, and ginger to canary, apricot, and bronze. Their long, curved beaks gleamed with streaks of silver and their massive heads nodded with framing ruffs of orange-red and tangerine feathers. Each was nearly the size of an ostrich, with a long, slender neck, and small, stubby wings. They sat on their perches in such perfect stillness, it was no surprise she initially mistook them for idols carved in stone.

Bonnie Mary held her breath, afraid to rouse the creatures. The gargantuan fowl sat silently on their lofty perches, eyes half-closed, as if heedless of the younger birds toiling on the chamber floor below.

The word *toil* was no exaggeration of the activities of the common birds (for when surrounded by their massive nest-sitting counterparts with their huge lion-like ruffs, they hardly seemed quite so peculiar). The cavern resembled a factory, with a procedure that went as follows: First, the common, ruffless birds entered the chamber through holes in the walls and ceiling. These passageways presumably exited out to different openings in the caves along the side of the mountain, just like one Bonnie Mary and Madsea had used to get in. In their beaks these birds carried fish and crustaceans from all over the island; plenty of food for the rest of the flock, which remained in the cavern, eager to be fed.

What Bonnie Mary never realized was that the birds she was used to seeing about the island were of the female variety only. The full-grown males of the species were nest-bound creatures that never strayed far from this single cozy cavern. Their enormous size was of great use to them for sitting on large clutches of eggs, for the wider their bottoms were, the more eggs they could incubate at a time. Of course, the males' bulk was not the only thing that warmed the eggs of the orange birds to make them grow and hatch more quickly than those of other birds of their size. The heat given off by the lava pools was essential in providing the ideal temperature for speedy incubation.

There were also smaller males about the cavern, with patchier ruffs than the giants sitting upon the nests. These males were younger and more active. It was one of these young males that sauntered by Bonnie Mary at that moment, carrying what looked for all the world like a shiny silver boot buckle in its beak.

Bonnie Mary watched the strange little creature with undisguised curiosity. *What in the world would a bird want with a boot buckle?* she thought.

With the buckle in its beak, the small male hopped over to one of the lava pools. It transferred the buckle to its talons and then, clasping its precious piece of metal tightly, proceeded to flap awkwardly over the boiling lava.

As Bonnie Mary watched, it stretched out the claw that held the buckle and plunged it straight *into* the boiling liquid. It held its claw there, wings beating frantically to stay in place. After a few seconds the bird pulled the object out. It went on to repeat the process until the metal held between its smoking claws was suitably soft and malleable.

Then, still holding the half-melted metal in its talons, the bird flapped clumsily over to a small, shining mound of metal and pressed the drooping, half-melted piece of silver into its surface. The determined little bird pushed and prodded the piece carefully into place with its beak and claws, smoothing it out like an expert metallurgist, until the new addition to its nest was as uniform in shape as the rest.

As Bonnie Mary observed this industrious young avian and its companions at work, she began to comprehend the purpose of this bizarre behaviour. Bonnie Mary recognized part of a half-melted ruby tiara sticking out of the nest. Instantly she knew what'd become of all the loot they'd stored in the cave over the years. Piece by painstaking piece, each bird had improved its nest with their treasure, raising it just that little touch higher, making it just that tiny bit shinier, all in an effort to attract a female. In this half-lit cavern world, she could see that a nest had to be very large and very shiny to attract any attention at all.

In the beginning, the ancestors of the peculiar orange birds of the Nameless Isle had decorated their nests with shiny seashells and bits of beach glass. The recent generation's discovery of the pirates' treasure had changed all that. While they still used rocks to build their nests, they now coated these rocks with layers of melted gold, silver, and sparkling gemstones stolen piece by piece and year after year from the pirates' hoard. Each individual piece of precious metal had been laboriously smelted and pressed into place on the nests at great physical cost by the birds who now sat upon them, still reaping the plentiful mating rewards of the discovery years later — well worth the singed talons.

"Unbelievable!" Bonnie Mary exclaimed. She was unsure whether she felt awe or anger at what the strange creatures had done with her life savings. What could she say? She had to laugh. She'd certainly never expected to foil Fetz like this!

Madsea's eyes danced in the red glow of the lava pools. "Yes. Yes. Yes. It's all here. The treasure is all here!" The silver teeth in his mouth flashed as he approached one of the smaller nests. Arms outstretched, he welcomed the gold into his embrace like a long lost friend.

A large, rusty-ruffed male, cracked open a sleepy eye from its lofty position atop a towering nest. An odd feeling came over Bonnie Mary at this. With a clairvoyant's sense, she clearly pictured what Madsea was about to do and knew instinctively that disaster would soon follow.

"Don't," she advised him softly, trying to move her lips as little as possible. "Them birds — I don't think we should be riling them."

"Nonsense," snorted Madsea. "They're *birds*. Just stupid big birds."

"Birds or not, I think we best scarper."

"How like a woman's cowardice to fold at the slightest sign of danger. See? You're all alike at the core, even you, the great Captain Bonnie Mary Bright!" Madsea grasped the nest closest to him. It was one of the few empty ones in the chamber, the young male who should've been guarding it otherwise occupied with trying to woo a nearby female.

"If we could just get this blasted thing … off!" grunted Madsea. "Help me, Mary!" Madsea pulled at the nest, trying to dislodge it from the ground without Bonnie Mary's assistance. As he continued to yank at the nest, a cry of alarm rose from a nearby avian sentry. Other birds in the vicinity chimed in, and screams of outrage echoed through the chamber.

Sensing her cue to flee, Bonnie Mary turned and dove back into the tunnel. She ran up the steep slope toward the faraway entrance of the cave, never stopping to look behind her.

They're alive!

Little Jane's thoughts pumped along with her vigorous legs, Melvin thumping woodenly against her thigh, her heart beating in time to the joyous news as she ran.

"Wait!" cried Villienne, close behind her, but she had no time for caution.

The path up the mountain narrowed as it twisted between the rocks. Little Jane slid around a bend behind a large pointed boulder.

She heard sounds of panting and groaning. At first she assumed it was an injured animal, but as she rounded the corner she realized her error. On the path lay an unmistakable human form of indeterminate gender covered in dust and spattered with blood. It sobbed and snuffled with its nose to the ground, the top of its grey head facing her as she moved cautiously forward. It heaved suddenly, throwing off a shower of black rock dust as it arched its back.

Little Jane watched as what she could now see was a man tried to push himself up on trembling arms, broad sailor's hands splayed in front of him. She saw the letters tattooed on his knuckles just as he managed to raise his head.

They read HOLD FAST.

Raising one cheek from the dust, Long John glanced up to see blurry human forms moving toward him. He thought they were the sailors from the *Panacea*, come for him at last, and resigned himself to his fate. He was too tired and hurt to even think of getting away. He concentrated on focusing his eyes, and the multiple figures coalesced into a single image of Little Jane, arms flapping willy-nilly about her as they always did when she ran. He smiled at the precision of the illusion. Perhaps Providence had seen fit to grant his final wish after all. He reached out a hand to the wavering mirage, not expecting to touch it but wanting to all the same. The phantom Little Jane grew closer as he stretched out his arm. Then, quite unexpectedly, it barrelled right into him.

"Papa!"

"Little Jane. Is it really you?" he rasped.

"Yes," she cried, wrapping her arms around him.

He buried his face in her braids, smelling the familiar tang of salt and seawater, and knew she was no phantom then. She was his beloved daughter, his own, his Little Jane! He cried with relief to see her unharmed. As her eyelashes touched his cheek their tears mingled, together at last.

Little Jane pulled away and through her tears stared in horror at the blood that trickled down her father's face. "Papa, you're hurt. What happened? Who did this to ..." Her voice cracked as she scanned his battered body.

"No, forget that. Listen to me, Jane. We've got to help your mother. He'll kill her. Help me up."

"No," said Villienne, who'd finally caught up. "You're in no condition, Silver." The magistrate bent gently over the injured pirate. "Just tell me where she is. I'll get her back for you safe and sound."

Thoughts tumbled unsteadily through Long John's rattled brain. "She's up there, up the path somewhere. Fetz ... Madsea's following her, heading up to the cave. It's the cave with the pear trees in front'a it —"

"Virgaleaus!" exclaimed Villienne excitedly. "I was right."

"Aye, aye," continued Long John impatiently, "the cave with a gold statue at its mouth. That be the one. Take this with you." Long John reached into the pocket of his breeches and removed the knife.

Villienne hesitated, seeing Kingly's blood still on the blade, but Little Jane's reflexes were faster. She grabbed the knife and ran.

"Little Jane, stop!" Long John yelled as she flew up the path. "Come back!" His hand tightened on Villienne's wrist. "Villienne, please. Go after her. She's just a girl. He'll hurt her if he catches her! Leave me here. I'll be a right."

But though Little Jane heard her father's words, she didn't stop. She sprinted onward, the knife flashing in her little hand, Melvin still bumping on her thigh, running faster than she ever had before.

Momma, hold fast, she thought, frantically. *I'm coming!*

Back in the bird's volcanic lair, Madsea turned as Bonnie Mary fled back up the tunnel. "Silly cow. Good riddance, ye rubbish!" he yelled after her. He had no need of the foolish woman now that the treasure was nearly his. He returned to tugging at the golden nest in earnest.

The peculiar orange birds grew increasingly agitated the more he tried to dislodge their handiwork. Their cries rose louder, echoing eerily off the walls of the chamber. Disturbed by the sound, small rocks began to fall from the ceiling, but Madsea was oblivious to all but the shiny nest. Orange wings beat the air behind him, but a swift wave of his hand frightened the birds away.

"Winged vermin!" he yelled. "What do you want with gold anyway? You're *birds* for Pete's sake."

Out of the corner of his eye he caught a glimpse of something big and reddish-orange, there one moment and gone the next. The flock squawked louder, emboldened by this apparition, but Madsea's fury only grew.

"It's mine by rights!" he screamed, his ragged voice overpowering their cries. "All those years I should've been pulling in the lucre. Get back!" Madsea swatted another bird away and gave the little gold nest another good yank. He was pleased to note it was beginning to loosen at last. Soon he would have it.

But a change had come over the deportment of the birds that even Madsea was beginning to notice. Their cacophonous cawing had ceased. The cavern was silent.

Like druids at a holy gathering, the orange birds stood about him now in a solemn circle. Their heads swayed in unison, their long beaks bobbing soundlessly up and down, up and down.

By the glow of the bubbling lava pools the rust-ruffed birds advanced together. Every bone in Madsea's body screamed at him to run, but he could not release the golden nest, not now that he was so close ...

"It's mine, mine by all what was done to me!" he shouted in frustration. "I earned it, not you." Tears wet his cheeks, but the peculiar birds only cocked their orange heads at him and blinked their beady black eyes.

Then he heard a sound from the back of the chamber, like many wings flapping in unison. In fact, the wings in motion were only two, but between them they contained enough feathers to cover a hundred smaller birds. As Madsea watched in disbelief, the immense creature separated itself from the deep shadows near the very top of the cavern, ponderously moving its bulk off the grandest nest in the chamber. Then, with a single squawk, it launched itself into the air. The other birds widened their circle, heads bowed low, as he descended among them, like some ancient titan of the avian race.

As Madsea stared, the creature landed with a ground-shaking thump on the floor of the cavern. It was old and ugly, and utterly enormous. The bird peered curiously at Madsea, fixing him with one huge obsidian eye as if he were a fresh morsel of food.

Unnerved by the creature's gaze, Madsea glanced down at its enormous claws, hideously twisted and burned from years of melting gold. Even with the sight of those terrifying claws, he refused to release his hold on the little golden nest.

All of a sudden, one of the smaller fledglings flew up awkwardly into the air and boldly landed on Madsea's arm, apparently eager to claim the nest's shininess for its own.

"Off! Off you foul thing," cried Madsea as he smacked the fledgling away. It flapped clumsily, trying to correct its flight path, but the little creature went careening off into the cave wall. It let out a pathetic cheep and slid to the ground, stunned. The other birds looked on as the young bird stumbled to its feet and tried to walk, trailing an injured wing.

A hundred pairs of eyes turned to glare at the intruder in their midst; the foolish man who'd dared to injure one of their most vulnerable members.

"Bird-brains," scoffed Madsea. "As if you lot had a single thought or feeling between you." Under the shadow of the giant bird, he began pulling at the nest again.

The beast clacked its massive beak once in warning and raised it to deliver the fatal strike. Then and only then did Madsea let go of the nest.

Bonnie Mary staggered out of the tunnel, blinking and sneezing in the sunlight, and saw the statue of Nakika, still standing sentinel by the mouth of the cave as always, just as if nothing had happened. She tried to wipe the dust and grime off her face. She suspected she had bird guano in her hair, but she didn't care. Giddily, she inhaled the fresh mountain air. At that moment, it tasted better than the finest of fine French wines.

It struck her as strange that she could still hear the eerie birdcalls and the faint flapping of ghostly orange wings even so far from the bird's nesting site. It was as if once heard, the sound could not be unheard, in the way that some awful sights, once seen, remain ingrained in one's mind forever. The sight of Jim's battered body, for example.

She knew she had to find him soon. If she didn't take him away from here, who knew what sort of carrion those birds might favour? With a shudder, Bonnie Mary turned away from the mouth of the cave ... and collided with something soft.

"Mama?" said a small voice.

"Little Jane?" With tears of delight and amazement, Bonnie Mary looked down and saw the face of her daughter. She clasped her tightly to her chest and kissed her dear little head a dozen times. Bonnie Mary held her so close that Little Jane soon found herself gasping for air.

"Oh, Little Jane," sniffed Bonnie Mary. "I were so worried about you. But what're ye doing here? Who brung you?"

"No one brung me." Little Jane laughed. "I brought meself! Ishiro and Villienne and them others all come along for the ride, but it was all me own idea. I'm here to rescue you, Momma. See," she added, brandishing Melvin the sword and the shiv knife with pride.

"The knife? But I gave that to your fa —" Bonnie Mary glanced anxiously about her. "Where's Jim?"

"Back down the path. I think he's hurt ... hurt bad."

"Oh," sighed Bonnie Mary, joy that Jim still lived vying with worry in her mind. "That stubborn fool. I shouldn't have left him. Come, Jane, show me where he be."

Little Jane took her mother's dusty hand in hers and together they began to pick their way down the steep path toward the spot where Little Jane had last seen her father.

As they came around the first sharp turn, they nearly ran straight into Villienne.

"Captain Bright!" exclaimed Villienne, grasping her hand in awkward greeting. "What a delight to find you looking so much better than your husband. I've so much to tell you."

"Later," Bonnie Mary interrupted him. "We'd best get outta danger and find Jim before Madsea do. Come!" Dazed, Villienne followed Bonnie Mary and Little Jane as they scrambled down the path.

"I just don't understand," protested Villienne as he stumbled after them. "What *is* this fellow's issue with you people anyway?"

"Revenge, for something what happen a thousand years ago, what weren't our fault even then," growled Bonnie Mary.

"Goodness!" Villienne frowned. "But where is this Madsea person now? I'd like to give him a piece of my mind, I would. He'd have to listen to me, you know. I *am* the magistrate. Is that why we're running? Is he chasing us?"

"*Was* chasing. Not anymore. Now it's the birds, them's what's chasing us." Bonnie Mary panted as she ran.

"Birds? Now I *really* don't understand."

Bonnie Mary swore as she tripped over an outcropping of rock. "Can you ever be quiet? I'll explain it all when we're back on the ship."

"Wait," interjected Little Jane. "He's right. We don't got to run away from the birds. You told me yourself the curse is all just rumours to scare people off the island. The birds ain't cursed as long as you don't try to eat 'em, right?"

Just as Bonnie Mary was about to explain to Little Jane how false that theory was, they heard a noise, like an explosion deep inside the mountain. Suddenly, in a shower of pebbles and black powder, a bizarre scarecrow of a man burst out of the cave in front of them.

Little Jane, Bonnie Mary, and Villienne stopped in their tracks and stared at the apparition who had appeared so suddenly.

The bleeding, dusty figure raised a single fist to the sky and screamed something that to Little Jane's ears sounded very much like "I'll get you for this, ye blasted Silvers!"

Chapter Seventeen

The Bird King's Revenge

"There must be more'n one tunnel out of there," moaned Bonnie Mary.

The skeletal stranger shook himself in a spectacular shower of black dust.

"Mum, who's that?"

"Fetzcaro Madsea," hissed Bonnie Mary, between gritted teeth. "He's the man what tried to kill us."

Little Jane stared in horror at the would-be murderer. He was covered in what looked like bird guano and clinging orange feathers. Angry red bite marks dotted his face and every unclothed spot on his body. Beneath that, Madsea's whole whippet-thin body vibrated with visible fury.

Madsea turned and saw them, and his hands balled into fists, the bloody beak marks standing out in fierce relief against his chalky white skin.

"It's you!" His voice broke in a strangled cry that ricocheted off the walls of the canyon below. "*You* did this. You and Jim. It was *you* what gave those birds the treasure. You led me in there to trap me. Scurvy liars, the lot of you!"

With a sudden show of strength Madsea leapt up over the rocks and took a wild swing at Bonnie Mary, but she managed to grab his wrist as it came at her, pinning it against the side of the mountain.

"Can't you see," Bonnie Mary shouted, "I ain't in control of them beasts! It ain't me, nor Jim, nor anyone human what carried off the treasure!"

Madsea thrashed as she struggled to keep his wrists pinned firmly against the rock. Villienne and Little Jane rushed to help; however, covered as he was in a slick coating of blood, guano, and feathers, Madsea managed to slip free. His foot connected with Villienne's stomach, sending the startled magistrate tumbling backward into Little Jane. They sprawled to the ground.

Bonnie Mary circled her foe, fists raised.

"Liar! You and yer sodding husband," Madsea screamed as he struck out at Bonnie Mary, coming at her from her blind side. Instinctively, she raised her arms to protect her face, giving Madsea the chance to land a kick to her belly with the spiked sole of his climbing shoe.

Little Jane blanched in horror.

"Ha! Now let her see you for what you really are. I'll show you —" he began, but fell silent as he felt something sharp jab into the small of his back.

"You leave me Mum alone!" shouted Little Jane as she pressed the blade into the fabric of his shirt.

"Oh, really?" Madsea gave a phlegmy, liquid laugh. "Is this the best you can do, little girl?" With a movement too fast for her to counter, he twisted away, nearly tearing the blade from her hand. "Have at me then."

"Remember, you asked for it," warned Little Jane. And then, for the first time ever outside fencing practice, she said the words she'd waited her whole life to say: "En garde, coward!"

With the shiv in one hand, she drew Melvin from the sash around her waist with the other. She lunged, and the sword's blunt wooden tip connected hard with Madsea's narrow chest, causing him to stagger back.

Little Jane willed her muscles to relax, adopting the crouched, ready posture Jezebel Mendoza had taught her. Her gaze darted from Madsea's eyes to his knees and back again. That was where the strike would come from, Jezebel always said. You see it first in the eyes and second the knees, ready to spring forward. Last in the hands, prepared to deal the blow.

She tensed as she waited for the first signs of Madsea's attack, but he remained where he was, as if frozen to the spot.

"Well?" she exclaimed impatiently. "Have at thee then."

An expression of terror fell over Madsea's narrow features and Little Jane realized, with a start, that he was truly frightened now. Frightened of *her!*

"Not just a little girl in pants *now*, am I?" she countered boldly, moving to strike him again.

However, Madsea seemed distracted, mechanically parrying her blow, not hearing her words. Taking advantage of his momentary lack of concentration, Little Jane moved in closer, the knife firm in her sweaty grasp. Even now, as she prepared for the final strike, she couldn't help but notice how his eyes refused to focus on her. Instead, they appeared to gaze up in rapt attention at something *behind* her. Little Jane raised the shiv, but hesitated. Something was not right. With mounting horror, she realized it must be someone other than herself who had Madsea so petrified. And if *Madsea* was so scared of this person …

Even though she knew it could give him the tactical advantage, Little Jane had to see what manner of man had terrified him so. She turned around and found herself staring into the black eyes of the largest bird she'd ever seen. Its enormous body nearly blocked the entrance to the tunnel Madsea had just emerged from.

Little Jane froze and, in her fright, did what Jezebel Mendoza told her never to do — she dropped her sword.

Luckily, Bonnie Mary had the presence of mind to pick Melvin up. "Back away slow," she whispered to Little Jane over her shoulder. "Don't go startling it."

Little Jane edged carefully backward, just as her mother instructed. But Madsea stood motionless, as surely as if he'd grown roots. The enormous bird slowly began to advance on him, clacking its immense beak.

All of a sudden Little Jane heard the sound of wings flapping. A small orange bird appeared at the entrance to the cave. More birds followed, and still more birds. Soon they poured forth from the abyss in a geyser of screaming orange feathers. Their cries split the air and their claws struck the ground, sending stones and dust flying up all around them.

"Get behind me, love!" shouted Bonnie Mary. Little Jane moved behind her mother and watched as, with one graceful sweep of Melvin, Bonnie Mary whisked a tide of birds away from them. Little Jane glanced around and was relieved to spot Villienne a little ways down the path, pelting his avian assailants with specimen jars from his pack.

Luckily, Villienne's specimen jars proved curiously successful weapons against the birds, as their bright, reflective surfaces were an ideal distraction. Whenever a jar broke, the birds couldn't resist fighting for even the tiniest shard of sparkling glass.

"Take that!" shouted Villienne triumphantly as he smashed the jars on the rocks all around. "And that!" Soon enough, though, he realized his supply of jars would exhaust itself long before the orange birds did, for there seemed no end to the avian onslaught.

With Little Jane's gaze fixed on Villienne for the moment, a stealthy orange bird took the opportunity to peck at her hand, attracted by the glint of the knife.

"Stop it!" Little Jane pulled her hand away, still holding the weapon firmly. It flashed silver in the light and many bird heads turned, suddenly alerted to the existence of this previously overlooked shiny object. They immediately converged on Little Jane, mad with desire for the glittering item.

"Mummy, help!" shrieked Little Jane as the birds swarmed over her.

Wielding Melvin like a scythe, Bonnie Mary slashed away at the birds, knocking them off Little Jane, but there were too many for her to repel completely. One tough little avian managed to propel itself up and under the arc of Bonnie Mary's arm. The creature pecked at Little Jane's fingers and the shiv fell from her hand.

Before the cry of pain even burst from her lips, the birds were upon the shiny knife, screeching, fighting for possession of the object with lusty beaks and clawing talons. Little Jane leapt back, taking cover behind a large rock. She scanned the scene before her, trying to find her mother and Villienne in the melee. The harsh sound of ripping canvas caught her attention. In horror she watched as two birds, trying to get at the valuable specimen jars at their source, seized the sides of Villienne's knapsack. Though it was still attached to his back by the shoulder straps, they slashed at it with vicious talons until it tore open.

"My precious samples. No! Desist, you harpies." Villienne swung at the birds as they pulled at his knapsack, but there were too many of them. They made fast work of the bag, rending it apart down the seam. The remainder of its shimmering glass contents tumbled out and shattered on the rocks, kicking off another avian frenzy.

"Stop! Stop! Do you know how long those took me to collect?" yelped Villienne, trying to wave them away with his hands. Little Jane could see it was a useless gesture, as new birds just flocked to claim the shards as soon as he'd shooed the old ones away.

At least they seemed to forget all about attacking Little Jane, Bonnie Mary, and Villienne in their passion for the pieces of glass. Little Jane breathed a sigh of relief as her mother grasped her hand behind the boulder. *Safe at last.*

Unfortunately, it was at precisely that moment that the enormous bird, which Bonnie Mary had come to think of as the Bird King, made its ponderous full exit from the mouth of the tunnel. With the entrance at last completely unblocked, the larger birds were free to emerge at last, and they spewed from the tunnel in an endless stream of fury.

"Hit the deck!" screamed Bonnie Mary, and though there was no actual deck to hit at the moment, she pulled Little Jane down to the ground with her. The air burst around them in an explosion of beating wings, clawing talons, and snapping beaks.

Dozens of the enormous birds that Bonnie Mary had seen in the cavern, too big and slow to make it off their nests for the first push, brought up the rear. In the nesting cavern they'd seemed such sleepy, slow-moving creatures. But no longer. Like a fire, slow to kindle, now raging out of control, they streamed forth, streaks of furious orange against the black of the cave's mouth.

And *still* Madsea stood there. Silver talons clawed the air above his head. Mighty beaks clacked around him. Yet in the strange realm that constituted the mind of Fetzcaro Madsea, there reigned a curious, unaccounted for feeling of peace and pleasure.

Madsea felt fine, seriously fine. For the first time in over a dozen years, he could breathe, really breathe, without coughing, gasping, expectorating blood, or even spitting out a single glob of phlegm. In fact, he realized he hadn't felt so fit for some time.

His lips formed a stiff line of determination. All he had were his fists, but with such newfound health coursing through him, he felt strong enough to take on the entire French navy. Soon he would have those golden nests. Nothing could stand in his way.

He laughed and caught a sharp look from the strange little girl in pants who had pulled the knife on him moments before. Then the creatures came on, streaking out of their dank den into the brilliance of the sun.

Swiftly, Madsea launched himself at the nearest orange bird with a flying roundhouse kick guaranteed to send a stout man straight to dreamland. Unfortunately, in his sudden glee at his newfound health, Madsea forgot two crucial facts: One, a bird is *not* a stout man. Two, the giant king of the peculiar orange birds was standing right there.

The enormous bird let out a shriek and flew at Madsea, its mighty silver beak opening wide like a great pair of scissors. Madsea had just enough time to jump back. The beak missed him by mere inches, fastening onto the tails of his coats instead.

Holding the fabric tightly, the bird pulled Madsea closer. Madsea loosed his arms from his coat sleeves and shrugged the garment off, leaving the incensed bird to toss aside the empty scrap of fabric. With all the strength in his scrawny, wasted arms, Madsea tried to pull himself up onto a large rock and out of the furious bird's reach.

He had almost made it up when he heard an angry cheeping nearby. Perched on the rock above him stood a small bird. It was sporting an awkward, dragging wing.

The tiny bird cried shrilly as it dug a pair of sharp little talons into Madsea's right hand.

Madsea creamed with pain and pulled his hand away.

The bird screeched again as it raked its talons across the back of Madsea's other hand. He pulled his left hand away from the rock, but, suddenly realizing he was no longer holding on to the rock with any hands at all, he fell in a heap to the ground below. Dizzily, he scrambled to his feet and tried again, pulling himself up on the massive boulder. He got his right leg up and over the rock, but his left leg dangled. Even dazzled by the unaccustomed brightness of the sun, the Bird King couldn't help but notice Madsea's leg squirming in front of him, looking very much like a giant, appetizing worm.

The bird's great beak opened again, sharp and silver in the light. Madsea tried to pull his leg away as the Bird King lunged straight for it.

Chapter Eighteen

The Power of the Seal

Villienne had helped Long John hop up the path as far as he could before he had run off after Little Jane (at Long John's insistence). After several unsuccessful attempts to stand on his own, the proud pirate had resorted to the indignity of crawling, dragging his injured half-leg behind him. He had to reach his family. But his progress was too slow for his liking, and he tried once more to stand. He hopped forward a few times, tripped, fell on a bed of green lichen, and blacked out.

When he came to, he heard screams and what sounded like hundreds of screeching birds. It took him a few minutes to realize that he'd landed on a ledge that jutted out over the steep cliff. Had he not been dizzy to start with, he certainly would have been as he gazed down at the azure curve of the moat sparkling cheerfully up at him, the serrated fangs of pointy black rock rising behind it.

As carefully as he could, Long John began to roll away from the edge. Aware that he was dangerously close to both the precipice and creeping unconsciousness, he used his fear of the former to prevent him from slipping into the depths of the latter.

The sounds of screams and screeching birds got louder and louder as he rolled. As he reached the path, the first person he saw was Bonnie Mary. With a sword in her hand and Little Jane at her side, she swiped away the swarm of orange birds that flapped around her in unbelievable numbers.

Unable to reach them, Long John could only watch as the incompetent magistrate tried his best to help them. Expecting the worst of Villienne, he was surprised to see the magistrate hold his own against the birds as Bonnie Mary and Little Jane rallied their forces to escape to safety behind some rocks.

Then Long John spotted Madsea. He was struggling to climb a large boulder, desperate to get away from the largest and most peculiar bird he'd seen in all his life. The bird's head swayed back and forth on its long, stalk-like neck as it prepared to strike. Madsea's legs dangled off the rock as he tried to wriggle up onto the ledge and out of the grasp of the bird's massive beak.

As the beak opened like a pair of enormous silver scissors, Long John closed his eyes and waited for the horrible snap of bone.

But then something quite unaccountable happened. Amid the dusty scuffle Long John heard a familiar voice shout "No!" Long John opened his eyes and craned his neck to try to see over the rocks, but all he could tell was that something was preventing the bird from lunging at its prey. Something or someone seemed to be holding it back.

Suddenly, Madsea lost his precarious grip on the boulder and fell. The giant bird lunged again, but once more came up short, screaming and struggling against whatever was holding it back.

As the bird twisted around, Long John saw Doc Lewiston, of all people, holding tight to the furious bird's tail feathers, keeping it from striking the final blow it needed to finish Madsea off.

The bird's head turned on its long swanlike neck to get a good look at its assailant. Lewiston let go of the bird's tail feathers, and the Bird King staggered backward and fell in the dust with an undignified squawk.

"Captain, quickly, before it can recover," Doc Lewiston shouted at Madsea.

Madsea groaned and crawled toward the doctor.

Lewiston snatched up the captain. Despite his new-found vigour, Madsea was still as light as a feather, and he sagged into unconsciousness. With the captain in his arms, Lewiston dashed behind the tall rocks near the edge of the path. Long John watched as the giant bird blinked and looked around, searching for the men.

Then the wings and bodies of more orange birds came between Long John and his view of the Bird King's attack. Even Little Jane and Bonnie Mary became difficult to distinguish amid the struggling masses of orange, though for a brief moment he *did* manage to catch a glimpse of Villienne. The embattled magistrate stood surrounded by more birds than Long John could count, all of them after the shards of broken glass scattered around him. His knapsack had already been torn to pieces by this point, leaving him reduced to bravely trying to whip the creatures away with what few strips of canvas remained.

"Look here," Villienne scolded the impervious orange birds. "I'm a card-carrying member of every scientific, natural, historical, and biological society in Britain. Trust me; you don't want an unflattering species designation from the Royal Society!"

Villienne took a whack at one of the birds with a vivid scarlet ruff. It wheeled away, momentarily stunned, but quickly recovered and circled back toward him, a creature with a mission. With needle-sharp talons outstretched, the bird dove at Villienne, determined to get at whatever shiny objects he might still be hiding.

Sensing the tide of battle about to turn against him, Villienne jumped back.

Though failing in its mission to acquire more shiny objects, the vengeful bird *did* manage to tear off a large piece of Villienne's shirt. With a cry of victory, it rose into the sky, carrying a scrap of monogrammed white linen away as a trophy.

Soon the rest of Villienne's shirt fell about his ankles in shreds, leaving the unimpressive breadth of his chest exposed to all the world.

As Villienne's narrow torso caught the light, the heads of all the peculiar orange birds in the vicinity swivelled in his direction like puppets controlled by a single string. For some bizarre reason they appeared mesmerized by the sight.

Little Jane saw the sea of orange bird heads turn ominously toward Villienne. Rarely exposed to the elements, Villienne's chest was as white as the underbelly of a frog and nearly as hairless. But it was not the paleness of his chest that so attracted the peculiar orange birds. There, for all to see, hung the symbol of royal officialdom, the British magistrate's Seal of Office. The golden disc reflected every ray of the golden afternoon sunlight off its scrupulously polished surface. Silence descended over both humans and birds, as if, for a moment, everyone was under a spell.

Then Little Jane was struck by a moment of inspiration.

Year after year she'd watched those birds as they flocked to the *Pieces of Eight* to perch upon its masts and railings. She knew them intimately; knew what they feared, knew what they wanted. And now, finally, she knew *exactly* how to give it to them.

"Villienne!" she shouted. But he remained frozen to the spot, stunned by the countless pairs of eyes staring fixedly his chest.

"Villienne," Little Jane repeated. "Throw it to me."

"Throw what? This?" he asked, holding up the empty straps of his torn bag.

"No. Not the bag. The seal!" Little Jane shouted, exasperated. "Throw me the magistrate's seal!"

"Oh, the seal." Villienne lifted the gold chain over his head. "Ready?" he bellowed back at her as the squawking began.

"Ready!" she yelled. "Now!"

Villienne hurled the disc directly at Little Jane. She watched it fly through the air, worried that Villienne's throw would fall short, but on this one day, Villienne threw with perfect accuracy. Little Jane caught the seal before a single orange bird could touch it. She turned and faced the edge of the cliff. Aiming for the gap between two large rocks, she threw the seal as hard as she could.

But hard as she threw it, the wind and her height worked against her, and the seal did *not* go flying over the edge of the cliff as she intended. It was *her* throw, not Villienne's that came up short.

Little Jane gasped in horror as the gleaming medallion hit one of the boulders and bounced back onto a patch of green that bordered the edge of the cliff. The seal rolled on its side in a dizzying circle, before coming to rest just feet from the edge.

With covetous shrieks the creatures lunged after the golden seal. Little Jane, Bonnie Mary, and Villienne rushed forward, but the birds were much faster. To everyone's surprise, however, the magistrate's seal was not the only thing that had come to rest in that particular patch of green.

With the last of his rapidly dwindling strength, Long John pulled himself forward, heedless of everything save the gold circle of the magistrate's seal, expanding before his eyes like a brilliant yellow sun. He stretched out one trembling hand and grasped it. Then he turned toward the cliff and, with a flick of his wrist, tossed the seal over the edge. The medallion flew out over the edge and disappeared from view. Wasting no time, the frenzied birds dove after it, down into the chasm.

Long John flattened himself against the ground, pressing his cheek against the soft lichen as they rushed past. He closed his eyes, trying to imagine he was sinking into the mountain, being absorbed by the rock itself, ignoring the awful brush of wings across his back.

The birds flew straight off the cliff in a thick knot of feathers, pushing and shoving, screaming and scrawing as they went.

Bonnie Mary turned away from this spectacle to glance back at the mouth of the cave, where several of the larger birds stood silently flanking the Bird King. The large bird looked down its long beak as if it disapproved of the undignified frenzy of the smaller birds, which could still be heard fighting over the seal.

As Bonnie Mary watched, the bird cocked its massive head toward her, wrinkled eyelids blinking over its deep, inky black eyes. At that moment, she could've sworn the creature understood her. She realized, with some amusement, that she'd unconsciously straightened her posture as if under another captain's scrutiny.

As one veteran fortune-hunter to another, Captain Bonnie Mary bowed respectfully to it. It should have felt ridiculous, but somehow, under these circumstances, it seemed the right thing to do. *And why not?* she thought. They were both captains, weren't they? Hardy survivors of a mad lifelong hunt for gold and fortune.

To her surprise, the Bird King returned her spontaneous gesture of regard, dipping its own massive head in response. This manoeuvre concluded, with a single *clack* of its beak the bird turned toward the mouth of tunnel.

The injured fledgling squawked loudly and jumped down on its elders' back just as the largest of the peculiar orange birds dipped its head and disappeared back into the tunnel from whence it came, followed by its entourage.

As she watched them vanish into the shadows, Bonnie Mary suddenly remembered Jim. She ran over to kneel beside him.

"Jim! Jim! Are you all right?"

Chapter Nineteen

Doc Lewiston's Oath

"Jim?" Bonnie Mary repeated.

He didn't answer her, but at least he was still breathing. Bonnie Mary steeled herself. Time for strategy, not emotion; she was the only captain conscious now.

"Pick him up," Captain Bonnie Mary Bright ordered Villienne brusquely. The magistrate did as she said, staggering a little under the pirate's weight. "C'mon, Little Jane." Obediently, Little Jane followed her mother and Villienne, her comatose father slung over his shoulder, down the path.

Suddenly, Doc Lewiston stepped out in front of them, Madsea slung across his back like a sack of potatoes.

"What are you doing with him?" Bonnie Mary scowled. "Leave him here."

"I can't," confessed Lewiston. "I know what he's done, but I'm ship's surgeon. I owe my oath to the captain and crew."

At this comment, Little Jane and Bonnie Mary swore some choice oaths of their own, but Lewiston stood his ground, refusing to relinquish his captain.

In the end Bonnie Mary made no move to stop the doctor. Exhausted as she was, she had neither the energy nor the time to argue with him. She was anxious to make it down to the rock bridge before nightfall, when it would be fully submerged by the incoming tide. As it was, they barely made it down the mountain in time.

As they reached the bottom, they ran into Darsa and the unstoppable Kingly. The two men were only too happy to head back to the ship with them.

The group traversed the rapidly disappearing rock path across the moat as quickly as they dared. By this time the sun hung low in the sky, providing just enough light for them to get back safely.

"Listen, Mama," whispered Little Jane as they edged along the narrow bridge, taking care not to fall on the slippery stone. "What's that?"

Bonnie Mary stopped to listen, but heard nothing other than the laboured breathing of the men behind them.

"The cannons, they've stopped firing!" exclaimed Little Jane. "Maybe Ishiro's won."

"I wonder ... could it be true?" whispered Bonnie Mary.

But before the two of them could wonder much more, the silhouettes of two figures appeared ahead of them on the shore.

"Jonesy!" cried Little Jane. "We left him behind when we tried to swim the moat," she explained to her mother.

Bonnie Mary squinted at the figures. "Aye, but who's that beside him?"

"All my days!" Little Jane laughed as she realized just who Jonesy's companion was. "It's Ned Ronk. And Jonesy's got 'im all tied up. "

And so two more members were added to their party.

The *Yorkman* and the *Panacea* were anchored close to shore, right near the old masthead. Both vessels were under the control of Captain Ishiro. The *Panacea*, though much damaged from her battle with the *Yorkman*, had remained afloat thanks to the concerted efforts of the *Yorkman*'s crew at bailing her out. With a few rough patches to the biggest holes in the hull, she was rendered able to be towed back to Jamaica.

Ishiro greeted his exhausted friends by the last light of the setting sun, his silver-black ponytail snapping behind him like an elegant silk pennant in the breeze, his old face lit with an unaccustomed smile, looking younger than he had in years.

"Ishiro!" exclaimed Bonnie Mary. "Mercy, but you're a sight for sore eyes."

Little Jane ran up to hug him, but when Ishiro reached out to embrace Bonnie Mary, she collapsed from exhaustion in his arms.

Slowly, Ishiro eased Bonnie Mary onto a packing crate before she could faint clean away.

"Jim," she said, oblivious to her own weakened state. "Tell me … how does he fare?"

Once he had seen to stout chains for the grumbling Ned Ronk, Jonesy went to help Villienne lay Long John out on the deck. Little Jane tried to help, but they shooed her away. She stood by the railing, nervously twisting a button on her shirt, unable to help as they examined her father.

Feeling sturdy wood planking beneath him once more, Long John stirred briefly into consciousness.

"Papa, I'm here!" cried Little Jane, rushing to her father's side.

Pushing Ishiro's arm away, Bonnie Mary stumbled across the deck to where Little Jane already knelt beside her father.

"Papa, c'mon." Little Jane squeezed her father's calloused hand. "Say something."

At last he opened his eyes. "Little Jane, Bonnie Mary," he nodded casually to them, as if he'd just strolled through the door of the Spyglass after a hard day's work, looking for a pint. "Good evening."

It was the last thing he said for two whole days.

Chapter Twenty

The Return

Madsea awoke with a start to find himself in the hold of a strange ship. He was lying in a box-bed under a foul-smelling blanket. His head hurt terribly and his body stung all over from bird bites too numerous to count. The last thing he remembered was the massive beak of the giant orange bird coming straight at him.

Struggling against the drowsiness that threatened to pull him back under, Madsea whipped the blanket off. He closed his eyes, steeling himself for whatever hideous unpleasantness might meet them. Experimentally, he shook his feet. They were clad in iron shackles fastened to a ring in the wall, but otherwise appeared to be, miraculously, unharmed. He reached up to touch the bandage that was wrapped around his head. His fingers came away sticky and he noticed they were covered with noxious-smelling green paste. Not too bad, all in all, he thought.

But just you wait until Mary and Jim get through with you!

That was assuming his old nemesis had survived, that is. Madsea was an old hand at the system of retributive justice practised among pirates and privateers. Though he'd never believed the world was a place kind or fair to its human inhabitants, he still saw it as fundamentally balanced in its own ruthless way. *The globe is a perfect sphere, after all,* he thought. Underneath the deceptive decorations of flowery words like *faith* and *brotherhood* the simple rule of symmetry still held sway. What Jim did to hurt Fetz so long ago caused him to hurt Jim in return, and now it was Jim's turn to even the score. *Nothing for it. It's just The Way the World Works,* thought Madsea bitterly, pausing for a moment of self-pity.

Except, no matter what popular globes may tell you, the world is neither perfectly spherical nor symmetrical, but fat around the middle and flattened at both poles. And last I checked there are several people on the planet who hold no truck with Madsea's view of The Way the World Works, and they're alive and well and going about their day to day business, all the same. Still, as a wealthy globe-maker once told me, generalizations are *so* much easier to construct.

Little Jane understood some things that Madsea, despite all his years of sailing and revenge, did not. Although she knew that, generally speaking, birds were colours other than orange, mothers weren't sea captains, and fathers had one hat and two feet, instead of one foot and many hats, the world was filled with ample proof that just because something happen in one way most of the time, didn't mean it *always* did or always *would*.

Then again, sometimes the pattern of a friendship, lost for a time, can return to our lives just when we least expect it. On the deck of the *Yorkman*, two old friends stood together watching the stars come out, carefully marking the position of the constellations in their notebooks, just as they once used to.

As had always been the case, Villienne took the fewest notes and talked the most between them, bursting with conversation as if he'd been storing it all up in their years apart. Doc Lewiston was pleased to listen to his old friend's wild, hopeful schemes concerning the beneficial purposes they might put the discovery of the green lichen to once they presented their findings to the learned societies of Britain. It was certainly a pleasant change from the insults he'd grown accustomed to taking from Madsea.

Thinking of his old captain once more, Lewiston reminded himself to check on him as soon as they were finished stargazing. The doctor was a tad concerned about what state of mind he'd find Madsea in once he emerged from his medicinal stupor. He was certain Madsea would be incensed at his capitulation to the enemy. He was glad he'd have Alistair Villienne there by his side to take his part when he went to confront the man. Even chained as Madsea was, the cruel force of his words could cut quicker than a surgeon's scalpel.

Later that night, Lewiston found himself sitting on a stool at Madsea's bedside, a teacup and saucer balanced precariously on his knee in precisely the same way he'd sat so many times back on the *Panacea*.

Had the room not been so different, Madsea might have sworn he was back there again, his strange sojourn upon the Nameless Isle no more than another fever dream. But then, there was the strange fact that for the first time in months he didn't feel the slightest bit feverish. Then the image of the monstrous bird bobbed unexpectedly to the surface of Madsea's thoughts. Could it really have been Lewiston who saved him? he wondered. It seemed impossible that this plump, persnickety little physician could have risen so dramatically to his rescue. And yet he remembered the gleam of spectacles flashing in the light just before the bird tried to bite him.

"You saved my life," Madsea said. "Why?"

"You're my patient and my captain. How could I not?" Lewiston replied with a gentle clink of teacup against saucer.

"Actually," said a voice from the head of the bed, "that wasn't the first time in the past few days either. Don't tell me you haven't noticed the recent improvement in your health."

"And just who the deuce are you?" Madsea glanced irritably around to locate the source of the mysterious voice.

"Sir Almost-Doctor Alistair Florence Virgil Villienne at your service. You have Lewy here to thank for your continued existence and also something else. Voila!" Villienne stepped out of the shadows flourishing a clump of green lichen. "I call it *lichenus nameless islenus*. What I believe it to be is the most powerful antibiotic agent ever discovered."

"Auntie what?" asked the irritated captain.

"Anti-bi-ot-ic," repeated Villienne slowly. "Means it kills germs."

"Germs?"

"Tiny animalcules invisible to the naked eye that cause disease," interjected Doc Lewiston.

Villienne gave their patient an encouraging smile. "Wondrous strange, this world we live in, isn't it?"

"Tiny invisible animals that cause disease?" scoffed Madsea. "That is without a doubt the stupidest thing I've ever heard."

"It's a new and fairly controversial theory," confessed Doc Lewiston. "I admit, even I wasn't certain of it until Villienne showed me his microscopic findings. Your recovery is proof that there's something in this plant, a chemical perhaps, that's poisonous to disease-causing organisms. We were wondering if you'd give us permission to write you up in a scholarly paper to present before the Royal College of Surge —"

"My permission? I'll give you no such thing," said Madsea haughtily.

"Whether you believe in the theory or not is immaterial," retorted Villienne. "This lichen saved your life, just as my friend Lewy here did. Another man would've simply left you to your fate. You're in no position to refuse him. He could always give you back to the pirates, you know. It was only through Lewy's pleading the importance of your case to the advancement of medicine that they agreed to release you into our care at all. Who knows? If Lewy here was to say we were mistaken, they might hang you still. After all, you did try to kill them."

"*Tried* to kill? You mean Silver still lives?" groaned Madsea.

Doc Lewiston removed his glasses and pinched the bridge of his nose. "You really can't keep anything under your hat, can you Alistair?"

"Sorry." Villienne cringed apologetically.

"You oughtta be well grateful he lives," came a high voice from the darkened corner of the room. "If he died by your hand, I'd give you a taste of me knife you wouldn't soon forget."

A glint of silver flashed from the shadows.

"How many people are in this room anyway?" asked Madsea, scrambling up onto his elbows. He turned to stare at the girl who emerged from the corner. "Who *are* you?"

Little Jane blinked back at him with surprise. "You truly don't remember?"

"Wait — you're the child! The spawn of Silver I thought me men captured, but no—you're the real one."

The truth of his words being evident, Little Jane said nothing.

"If you're Silver's daughter," Madsea continued, "then you *must* know."

"Know what?" asked Little Jane, curious in spite of herself.

"What a liar he is. Whatever he told you about me, best believe it's pure fiction. He sold me out — me, the man he once called his brother. Glad I put him through hell on the island. Won't forget that beating soon, will he?" added Madsea with a malicious grin. "I'll die proud now that I've done that, whatever happens."

Doc Lewiston grimaced at his captain's twisted sentiments. Why *had* he saved the man?

"Sold you out? What in blazes are you talking about?" asked Little Jane.

"Your Silver's daughter, so you say. Then you should know your father betrayed me to the French at the battle of Anguilla. He sat there on the *Pieces of Eight* while my ship was blown to bits, leaving me for the French to capture. I near died of fever in their stinking prison, but I survived to take back what's mine by rights. He owes me my share o' the wealth he and your cursed mother stole from me, all they made while I mouldered away in that blasted prison. But somehow, someway, they tricked me. Gave it all to those bleedin' birds. Don't see how they arranged to do it, but —"

"Are you serious?" Little Jane interrupted his nonsensical tirade. "All this happened, what, fifteen years ago? They barely made it outta that battle alive themselves. Old Captain Thomas Bright were gut-shot and died. Go see his grave on the island, you don't believe me. Me mum took a sword hit to the face, for Pete's sake. Not the *Newton* nor the *Golden Fleece* made it back. Ask Ishiro how many men went down on *his* ship. If yer boat sunk under your command, it be *yer* fault. Me father had little time enough to lead a tactical retreat and save me mother, without wasting precious time tryin' to make up for your dodgy seamanship. If he'd rather save her than stick around and risk gettin' hisself and his ship stove-in trying to fish you out of the drink, who's to blame him for that?"

"Lies!" Madsea shook his head vehemently, trying to clear her sensible statements out of his mind. "I know the currency of your kind."

"Fine, I lie. To what purpose then? Ain't you ever bothered to check a history of the battle afore throwing all your scanty years away on this scheme? The records is all there in the governor's mansion. It's not secret."

"Records can lie, depends on the writer, what stories he's been listening to. Jim ever tell you what happened to his leg?"

"What's that got to do with anything?" asked Little Jane, confused by his abrupt change in conversation topics.

"Some heroic tale about taking a bullet for Admiral Rodney at Martinique?"

"Actually, I ain't heard that one."

"But you've heard *some* rubbish story, plain enough. Don't feel bad. I believed him once, too," confessed Madsea, "but rotting away in prison, I had time to smarten up. Y'see Jane, a person's either an honest man or he's a liar, and you know what sort your father is. A false thing through and through. A man like that lies about *everything*."

"No," said Little Jane in a small voice. "Not everything. The story he told me about the battle of Anguilla — that be none of his invention."

"And how d'ye know that?" asked Madsea with a sardonic smile.

"Weren't anything funny about it, fer one thing," replied Little Jane. She'd said it instinctively, but upon reflection saw the truth in her own words. She'd never in her life known her father to tell a completely serious story, yet when he'd talked of the battle and of the two ships and their men who had vanished into the foaming water before his eyes, he'd been grim from start to finish. The tears he hastily scrubbed away as he spoke of the loss of his childhood friend were real, not for show.

"It don't matter," coughed Madsea. "I still got me letter of marque. It gives me permission from the Crown. They're still identified as pirates by British law. If I don't get them, another pirate hunter will. If you make Jamaica or any other British colony with me ship, they'll just clap you all in irons and send you to prison."

Little Jane could only glare at him, knowing that was true.

"Maybe," said the magistrate, "and maybe not. Where's the letter now?"

"Down in the captain's state room on the *Panacea*, I imagine," said Little Jane. "But what difference—"

"Just lead me there. It's time I tested out a theory."

For two days, Long John lay in Ishiro's cabin floating in a pharmacological haze. Every two hours Little Jane and Bonnie Mary had been deputized to wake him to prevent his concussion from worsening.

Finally, Doc Lewiston decreed that Jim was out of the worst of the danger and the mixture of laudanum and green lichen powder was reduced enough to let him fully wake.

Had the smelling salts employed by Bonnie Mary not done the trick, the reeking stench of the green lichen poultices liberally applied to his wounds could have worked just as well. At least, Jim thought upon nearly gagging on the smell, no one had the temerity to break out the leeches.

Gingerly, he reached up to feel the bandage wrapped around his still-aching head. His nose felt like Ishiro had given it the once over with one of his meat tenderizers. Gazing into the small shaving glass by his bedside, he noticed someone had thoughtfully stitched up a gaping cut that ran across his right eyebrow with strands of coloured thread. Other than his concussed head, the broken knee of his short leg had suffered the brunt of the damage. Doc Lewiston had immobilized it in an awkward structure of wooden scaffolding and stiffened plaster while Long John was asleep.

On the plus side, his mind seemed none the worse for wear, despite a persistent, though fading headache, and his wounds remained pleasantly rot-free, even if they did stink of lichen. Most importantly, Bonnie Mary and Little Jane were alive and safe, and for that he would be forever grateful. Nothing could ever take the shine off that for him.

Yet, despite this, he could not rest easy. Part of him still couldn't believe what had transpired since his surreal reunion with Fetz aboard the *Panacea*. All the years since Fetz's supposed death, Jim had mourned his friend. It had comforted him to think that even if Fetz's life had not been long, it had been happy, at least during the years they had been shipmates together.

But now? He favoured the wooden planks of the ceiling with a grim twist of a smile. Now he wanted to kill Fetz for what he'd done. *Especially* for what he put Little Jane and Bonnie Mary through. For that, there was no forgiving.

Didn't matter that he couldn't walk. A person didn't need to get up to fire a pistol. One shot would be all it would take.

Idly, he reached around to finger the octopus tattoo on his back, the one Fetz'd given him, but it was hidden under too many bandages to touch. He thought of his father and how he'd scoff at this sentimentality. Too soft by far, he would say.

Maybe. *But look at what made Madsea strong.* Even if he hated Madsea now, he knew he couldn't kill him. Little Jane deserved a better father than one who'd do that. A person without pity wasn't what he wanted her to grow up to be, not if he had any say in the matter.

So maybe he wasn't ruthless like Long John the First. He could use his facility for imagination to think of other solutions. Wasn't that just what he'd been doing his whole life? After all, a good pirate was nothing if not resourceful.

The next time Long John awoke, Little Jane was sitting quietly by his bed.

"I weren't sure if you was sleeping," she said shyly.

"I'm awake now. What's your mother say 'bout our time to Jamaica?"

"Two or three days. The sea's becalmed and we're towing the *Panacea*, so Ishiro don't see no reason to push it."

"Good on him. Give the men some rest. They deserves it," he said.

Little Jane paused as she tried to remember what else she was supposed to say, so distracted was she still by her father's battered appearance. It made her furious, what they'd done to him. She looked away, trying not to let him see how much it distressed her.

"How's Jonesy?" he asked. "Still stuck over the side of a railing?" Long John smiled, trying to set her at ease, but she would not meet his eye. He touched her under the chin, raising her gaze to meet his. "I knows it looks a mite rough," he said softly, "but I'll be all right. Don't you worry. Old bones just don't heal fast as young is all."

His calloused fingers gently touched the palms of her hands. Much to Little Jane's surprise, she noticed the angry red rope burns she'd suffered weeks before had faded to unobtrusive white lines without her even noticing.

"Takes a lot more'n that to keep a Silver down," he said stoutly. "Now bring me sticks over," he instructed her. "'Bout time I were getting up."

"But, Doc —"

"No harm in me taking a quick turn 'bove decks. I been longing to see this fine ship ye got fer yerself anyway."

"Wait, about the *Yorkman*." Little Jane shifted uncomfortably. "What're we gonna do? I ain't told you, but it's not really ours. Villienne commandeered it off a shipbuilder. He won't let us keep it."

"Then we'll have to go back and return it just as the good magistrate says. Me and yer mum'll settle with the *Yorkman*'s crew, give 'em the rest of their fee and —"

"But what'll we do for gold to pay 'em with now that the birds' got it all?" asked Little Jane in despair. "Even say by some miracle we manages to pay the crew, what's left to us to buy food? Everything you and Mum be working for all your days, it's gone, all of it!" She glanced over at her father to gauge his reaction, but incredibly his mild expression remained unchanged. Maybe he was still on the laudanum, she thought. "I don't understand!" she exclaimed. "Don't it bother you none?"

"Perhaps it were true, it would," he said slowly, eyes twinkling. "'Course, who says it's all gone, at that?"

"But the birds —"

"Shhhhh!" Long John stopped the flow of Little Jane's words with a finger to his lips. "No point spreadin' it round, love, but we still got us a little gold what weren't on the island."

"What? Where?" she asked, glancing around the room, as if said gold would miraculously materialize from behind the crockery.

"First National Bank of Jamaica, that's where."

"Bank of Jamaica? But you always said bankers is all crooks and you don't believe in 'em. Worse thieves than us, you said. I heard it," she protested.

"True 'nough. But even we privateers got to be practical every so often. Come now, don't act so shocked. If we was ever in an emergency and needed money straight away, wouldn't it be a tad inconvenient fer us to go sailing all the way to the Nameless Isle to get it?"

"B-but you never told me before."

"Which were a mistake, I reckon, and not the only one I been making lately, but I'm thinking yer old enough now, time you knows these things. Me and yer mum just ain't wanted to frighten you, goin' on about wills and inheritances and such." He paused thoughtfully for a moment. "Though, I's surprised Jonesy never mentioned it to you while we was gone. I *did* tell him if anything ever happen t'me or Mary he were to make sure you knew it."

"Wait a tick. You told who?"

"Jonesy."

Little Jane smacked her forehead with the palm of her hand. "You entrusted the knowledge of your secret bank account to Jonesy?"

Long John scratched his cast thoughtfully. "Perhaps that weren't the most well-thought-out decision, now that ye mentions it. Not that he ain't a brilliant musician and barkeep," he added loyally. "The money ain't a lot, mind, but you know me and yer mum'd never leave you skint."

"I don't care anyway, Papa," she said. "I'm just glad you and Mum's back with me in one piece."

"Two pieces, in my case, I suppose," he admitted ruefully. "But me, too, Jane. Me, too."

"Speaking of Mum, where's she at? There's something Villienne wants to show us."

"And what's that?"

"No idea, says we'll like it though."

With a theatrical gesture Villienne removed a sheet of paper from a worn leather case and placed it on the side of Long John's bed.

"I don't understand. What is this exactly?" asked Bonnie Mary, confusion corrugating her brow.

At that moment she seemed to speak for nearly everyone gathered in Ishiro's cabin, which was by this time crowded near to bursting. Little Jane, Bonnie Mary, Long John, Ishiro, Villienne, Doc Lewiston, Jonesy, and Mendoza sat on the bed or stood staring down at the papers. Harley, Rufus, and Sharpova were there, too, although they had to look over everyone else's heads, as they were busy holding Fetzcaro Madsea and Ned Ronk between them in chains.

"What exactly is we supposed to be looking at?" asked Little Jane, peering down at the papers.

"Before you start," broke in Madsea, "I submit you've all forgot one crucial point."

"Yes, and what's that?" asked Long John testily.

"That unlike you lot, I'm an official privateer and pirate hunter for his majesty the King of England, and you —"

"But you're not," interrupted Villienne. "Look here." He pointed with a magnifying glass at the letter of marque. "You're not an officially licensed privateer at all."

"That's absurd!" cried Madsea, looking around at his assembled audience. "Who are you going to believe? Me or this paintbrush-handed idiot here?"

Villienne hid his stained hands in his pockets and looked down.

"Whatever he may look like to you," Little Jane growled at Madsea. "He's a right clever man and the justly appointed magistrate of Smuggler's Bay, and if he says it's so, then I thinks he's right. I don't believe you are an official pirate hunter." With that, she folded her arms over her chest, as if that settled the matter.

Long John put his hand to his aching head. "Would someone please explain this to me."

"This letter of marque here, it's a forgery," said Villienne simply.

Doc Lewiston glanced from Villienne to Madsea.

Madsea's face contorted with fury. "What d'ye know anyway?" he yelled. Ned Ronk shot his former captain a look that would pierce granite.

"I know," replied the magistrate coldly, "because for an entire year I wore the king's seal around my neck, and would be wearing it still if not for a recent incident involving a certain unmentionable species of bird. For a whole year, I polished that seal every morning after breakfast and every afternoon before tea, and this ..." Villienne tapped the impression in the wax at the bottom of the letter of marque. "This isn't it. This was made using an old cricket medallion."

"What?"

"See, if you look closely enough you can just make out the outline of a man with a cricket bat where it should be Lady Britannia with her shield."

Ishiro took the paper and placed it under the large magnifier they used for viewing navigational maps, thereby exposing its clearly cricket medallion nature to everyone.

"Ridiculous," scoffed Madsea, still trying to maintain his ruse.

"I know," marvelled Villienne. "I mean, how could anybody be tricked by such obvious fakery? It's so clearly a cricket bat, if they just bothered to really look."

Swearing, Ned Ronk strained at his chains, still trying to get close enough to choke his former captain.

"Why on earth would you need a fake seal?" Doc Lewiston removed his spectacles to rub his tired eyes.

"Don't you see," sighed Madsea. "I *tried* to get a king's letter to come out here, but the bleedin' Admiralty wouldn't give me a thing. All I could get was authorization to blockade merchant ships delivering supplies to revolutionaries in Massachusetts, and who wants to do that?" The pirate hunter let out a wretched sob. "Blast you, you've ruined my life completely now, Silver. If not for you, I wouldn't have spent all these years rotting away, dying of consumption. I'll have me vengeance yet!"

"Why?" Little Jane's voice broke through the quiet.

"Why?" Madsea gasped.

"I mean you're not rotting away dying of consumption anymore," said Little Jane sensibly. "Even then, all them years ago, you escaped. And what'd you do with the time? Went on some stupid quest to deprive a girl of her parents, that's what. You could've done anything … penned songs, painted pictures … 'stead you chose to do this."

"You —" Madsea began, but realized he could think of no suitable reply. He'd never thought of it in that way that before. Was it possible the girl was right?

"Let us say," said Bonnie Mary sweeping the papers off the bed, back into Villienne's capable hands. "That the *Panacea*, commandeered without the Crown's permission, was unfortunately sunk and the ship we're towing now is the *Pieces of Eight*, damaged from some encounter with the rocks around the Nameless Isle. Still more than salvageable with a little work and refitting, but looking a little different from her old self. That should suffice, I think," she added with satisfaction.

"After all." Long John smiled slyly. "You can't expect us to come out o' this with no compensation, now."

"But, my investors in London —"

"Ain't our problem," replied Bonnie Mary. "Though if I was you I'd keep me head down when Villienne and

Lewiston here shows ye off to all those bigwigs at the Royal Society."

"What about me?" asked Ned Ronk. "Me what served you and yer husband before the mast fer three good years —"

"And threatened to kill our daughter, after all our kindness to you, you cruel-hearted beast," snarled Bonnie Mary. "You and any what sticks by you from the *Panacea*'ll find yourselves a nice cozy berth on one of them lovely whaling ships sailing out to Antarctica, how about that? Any of us find you round Jamaica or any other of the islands, well, we ain't countin' ourselves responsible for our actions. Not to mention those of the authorities what might be pleased to hang a fella for what you done."

Long John glowered up at Fetz and Ned, unable to restrain his emotion. When he spoke, his voice was all the more chilling for its unaccustomed softness: "I'll show you mercy this time, but anyone of you or your crew *ever* hurt another person the way ye hurt me and my family — you ever even *think* on it — you'll come to regret it. I find you're up to tricks again, so help me, one night ye'll hear me step upon the stair and that'll be the last thing ye'll be hearing in this life again. You get me, shipmates?"

"Aye, aye!"

"Aye, aye what?"

"Captain Silver."

"Best be remembering that."

Chapter Twenty-One

Return to Smuggler's Bay

All told, Little Jane spent three months in Jamaica, helping her parents recover and repair their new ship. It had been a month since Villienne and Lewiston set sail for England with their captive research subject in tow, and she'd been chomping at the bit to leave ever since.

Oddly enough, she found she missed the magistrate now that he was gone. Somehow, in the course of their adventures together she'd grown quite fond of him. While he was in Kingston, she often found herself loitering around the laboratory, listening to him talk as she assisted him and Lewiston with their chemistry. She enjoyed watching Villienne's wiry frame quiver with energy as he spoke to her of his theories. Occasionally he'd even dance a jerky little jig step across the room when stimulated beyond mere verbal expressions of joy at the results.

For his own part, Villienne loved an audience. He could no more horde knowledge than a bucket could contain an ocean.

Little Jane noticed that Long John and Bonnie Mary, despite their gratitude to the scientists, cared little for how Lewiston and Villienne's discovery actually worked, unrelated to sailing or storytelling as it was. Secretly this pleased her. Her newfound knowledge of medicine, poetry, and explosives could remain her own unique store of power; like her voice, her own special *modus operandi,* as weaponsmaster Mendoza liked to say.

The day Villienne left, a gift was delivered to their rented rooms in Kingston. It was a blank book with a green leather cover to replace the one she lost on the *Pieces.* When Little Jane opened it, the title on the flyleaf made her smile: "How to Be a Good _____."

It was strange to stop dreaming about becoming an infamous pirate. All her life, that's all she'd ever wished for. She thought she might still want to be a sea captain, but not one like her parents. Smuggling and stealing for a living *did* seem to make people dislike you in some particularly nasty ways, she'd observed. Conceiving of her parents' profession like this was new to her, but after her recent experiences she could no longer think of it in the same light. Something within her had changed.

What surprised her even more was that her parents seemed to be changing, too. She'd overheard them in Kingston talking one night when she was supposed to be asleep.

"I been thinking, Jim," her mother began, ordinarily enough. "If this green lichen works as well curing others as it done wit you, might be an idea for us to make ourselves some profitable business outta it."

"How d'ye figure that?"

"What I been thinking," explained Bonnie Mary, "is there's got to be some way to harvest it, so's we could sell it. Villienne or Lewiston make it a popular treatment back in England, there's no telling what sort of price it'll fetch on market. We could hire some fellas to pick it off the island and make a fortune exporting as medicine, like was done with tobacco and rum."

"Makes sense I suppose, but d'ye really think we could make a go of it?" mused Long John. "Old seadogs like us, turning merchant?"

"No idea, but I guess it ain't so much different from what we be doing now. I mean, we're already pretty good at parting people from their money."

"That's true."

"Only difference is, if we was merchants, they'd get something for it in return."

"*And* they'd be less likely to try to shoot us," remarked Long John.

The two pirate captains lapsed into silence after this, each absorbed in his or her own thoughts. Much as an outlaw's existence still greatly appealed to their rebellious natures, they knew there came a day in every pirate's life when the risk of being shot and maimed on a daily basis began to lose its lustre. Perhaps *this* was that day.

"'Course that means we got to go back to the Nameless Isle to harvest the foul stuff," Long John added.

"Just think, you could take on one of them orange birds as a pet," suggested Bonnie Mary cheerily. "Train it up like that ornery parrot your mum used to keep. What was his-name?"

"Don't even say it," grumbled Long John.

"Captain —"

Little Jane heard her mother's husky, muffled laughter as her father threw a blanket over her head.

Then all was quiet and still, except for Little Jane's mind, which was suddenly running like a hamster on a wheel.

If this lichen trade took off, her parents might actually become legitimate merchants — a bizarre thought. Could they even take to that sort of life so late in the game? Realistically, Little Jane knew that day would still be a long time coming, if it ever came at all. Still, if the past few months had taught her anything, it was that strange things happened all the time.

The return of the new *Pieces of Eight* was occasion for much joy and celebration in Smuggler's Bay. On the night of their welcome-home festivities, Jonesy told Jane that he couldn't remember ever having been to a better party. Taking into account her cousin's considerable expertise in this area, Little Jane thought this high praise indeed.

The next day she greeted the dawn from the porch of the Spyglass, where she'd fallen asleep on the old swing bench the night before.

The ocean was wondrously calm, like a misty silver mirror. Now and then shifting rays of light broke through the morning clouds to trace yellowy patches on the water below. The only sounds to be heard were the call of the gulls wheeling by in the sky and the *scrip-scrape* of her father's carving knife, whittling away at a piece of wood. Sleepily, she listened to him whistling to himself, keeping time with the motion of the blade.

"What'chu makin'?" Little Jane asked, sitting up.

Her father jumped, startled by the sound of her voice. He'd been so engrossed in his work that he hadn't noticed she was awake.

"Shhhhh." Long John held a finger to his lips and gestured with a nod to Bonnie Mary, softly snoring at the other end of the bench.

Quietly as she could, Little Jane came over and climbed up beside him. He brushed some wood shavings aside and favoured her with a conspiratorial grin. She saw he held a fresh wooden peg leg in his hands, and that he had already started carving it.

"Well done," she whispered, squeezing his arm.

He turned the wooden column around, secretly satisfied with her approval. He continued carving as Little Jane nestled into his side, absorbing the warmth of his body.

She watched the morning light shine through the tendrils of her mother's hair as she slept, making a backlit halo of gold around her dark curls. Tucked up against her father's chest, Little Jane scrutinized his carvings. She recognized the old sailor's precautions against drowning; the proud rooster carved to match the pig tattooed on his ankle.

"Reckon it should keep me afloat a few years more," he remarked.

"Capital rooster," she complimented him, "but what's this other design?"

"Look closer," he said, eyes twinkling as she peered down. "Recognize it?"

Now she noticed a set of familiar jagged peaks etched in miniature around a little ring-shaped moat and finger-sized volcano; a precise, tiny map of the Nameless Isle. Skirting its edges were the words MASTHEAD EAST VERGALOO IN NAKIKA.

Little Jane frowned. She wasn't certain she approved of making the directional code to the secret treasure cave so obvious that anyone could see it, but then the secret treasure cave was technically no longer a secret, nor did it possess any treasure, for that matter.

Plenty of fresh, yellow wood remained bare, still unmarked by the knife. "What are you planning for those parts?" she asked.

"Got to have me some new adventures to carve, I guess," he said as he wiped the blade clean on his breeches.

"Or just think up more imaginary ones," Little Jane suggested as she rummaged through her pockets.

Distractedly, Long John kneaded his half-leg between his hands. It was still splinted and lightly bandaged, but no longer pained him as it had before. He still had a few months to go before he would be done with the crutches. He'd got new ones, of course, to replace the pair that had undergone various transformations into rowing oars, floatation devices, and clubs back on the Nameless Isle. He was still occasionally startled when he glimpsed his reflection out of the corner of his eye in a mirror, thinking for a split second it was Old Captain Silver come back again; but the resemblance had begun to amuse rather than disturb him. Now he just tipped his hat in greeting to the old rogue when he sidled by in the glass.

Little Jane rifled through her pockets removing odds and ends until she found what she was looking for. "Ah, there you are!" she exclaimed as she produced her battered old exercise book for him. The title "How to Be a Good Pirate" was still mostly visible despite the grubby condition of the cover, so different from her pristine new leather journal. It had survived much, this book, even more than Little Jane knew. "I was thinking I lost it when the *Pieces* went down, but yesterday, at the inn, Mum gave it back to me. When I asked her where she found it, she said you was keeping it safe for me, holding it all them days you was locked up. With the party yesterday, I clean forgot to tell you."

"Don't mention it. I been meaning to give it back to you for a dog's age," he replied. "Kept me busy when I were in the brig on the *Panacea*, it did. Thankee for that."

Little Jane cracked open the book's sticky cover, surprised to find all the pages that had been blank before she lost it now mysteriously filled with writing. She peered at the illegible scrawl, unable to decipher a word, though she thought she recognized the large hand it was written in.

"You?" she asked, perplexed. "You wrote this, didn't you?"

Long John nodded.

"Took up all me blank pages and wrote over the ones I wrote on, too?"

"Aye," he muttered sheepishly. "Kind of took to usin' it when I were prisoner. See, I were thinkin' to meself, I don't make it out, there's a few things about yer old father you might be wanting to know someday."

"What things?"

"Oh, just happenings and such," he continued with a vague wave of his hand. "Things maybe I ain't told you quite straight the first time round, you know?"

"Really?" Little Jane raised an eyebrow. She was sure she could fill several books with things he'd not told her quite straight the first time around.

"Had a chance to read it yet?" he asked casually.

"No. How could I?" She held out a scribbled page for his perusal. "Look."

It was one of the pages he'd written on during his worst night in the brig, that awful dark night that seemed to last for days. It was also completely illegible, even to him.

"Is it in code?" Little Jane asked, peering more closely at the page.

"No, it ain't code," he groaned. He thought of all that effort he'd put into writing his great confession down that horrid night and the result he saw before him now in the light of day: indecipherable words scrawled over more indecipherable words. In short, an illegible mess.

"Then why —"

"I were writing in the dark. Guess I've made a right mess of things again. Sorry, love. This last while you ain't exactly seen me at me best."

"Rubbish," she retorted. How could he forget that day on the island when he'd thrown the magistrate's seal off the cliff? "You and Mum saved me," she told him, "that day on the Nameless Isle. You was a hero. You saved us all."

"No, Little Jane," said Long John, looking her square in the eye. "It were *you*. You brought everyone together, went to call on the magistrate, scraped up all the money and rallied a crew to our cause. That were what saved us, Little Jane — and you should know there ain't nothing I'm more proud of in this world than having such a brave an' resourceful young woman for me daughter."

Little Jane flushed under this fulsome praise, not knowing what to say. Of all the remarkable things her father had told her over the years, this last was the most remarkable of all.

"I don't need to read what you wrote, Papa," she said softly.

"Oh," he replied, disappointed. "I thought you'd maybe want to know —"

"It's not that. What I mean is, we're both of us here now. You don't need to write it. Whatever it is, you can *tell* me."

It was true, Long John realized to his amazement. He really could tell her anything he wanted about his past now. Nothing would serve to contradict whatever fanciful heroic tale he spun. Fragmented fictions rushed through his mind, pliable shapes his nimble imagination could easily bend to whatever purpose he chose. He already had the beginnings of a cracking good yarn forming, a story of redemption and revenge, love and hate, pitched duels, witty jests and fair maidens …

He paused to look at Little Jane, his best audience, always. Expectantly, she gazed up at him, waiting for his story with all the patience her twelve-year-old body could muster. In the morning light he could clearly see each individual fleck of colour in the irises of her eyes. Somehow, despite all the slip-ups, mess-ups, cock-ups, and fess-ups, somehow, he realized, she was still willing to believe him. To believe *in* him.

Little Jane called him a hero and that was more than enough for him. He took a deep breath, still unsure how to begin. "For you and only you," he said, "I'll tell me tale straight as I meant fer you to know it when I wrote it down in the brig. But if it ain't what you thought, don't —"

"Wait." Little Jane interrupted him. "Before you start, there's something I need to tell you."

"What's that?"

"I want to change me name," she announced. "I don't want to be called Little Jane anymore."

"But —"

"I'm a proper sailor, just as much as anyone else round here. I ain't a passenger nor little girl in pants neither. I don't want the rest of them thinkin' I just be here on account of being the captains' daughter."

"What do you want then?"

"What I want," she said passionately, "all I ever wanted, were to count meself a real member of your crew. Just like you and Mum and all the rest."

"I don't understand." he narrowed his eyes. "Whoever said you weren't?"

Words tumbled out of her in a rush. "Ned said … the accident with the cannon … it weren't me … he just made it look like … the fabric-seller at the marketplace saying I'm just a girl in pants … those twins at the magistrate's mansion what wouldn't let me in, and made me go in a tub … looked at me sailor's tattoos and laughed … told them you was a cannibal and…."

Suddenly, she stopped herself.

Who *had* said those things about her? Charity and Felicity Dovecoat? Ned Ronk? Some random fabric merchant? No one she'd ever held in high esteem, that was certain.

"Oh, Jane. You always been a part o' this crew," Long John said, his voice quavering with emotion. "You know you was born on the *Pieces of Eight*. Ain't no one more a part o' her than you. Now what tar round here can say they's crewed a ship from *that* age? If you ain't fond of your name, then you've long since earned the right t'call yourself whatever you please. That suit?"

Little Jane nodded vigorously. "It suits me fine."

"Good. Now, you still wants to hear me story?"

"Come on, what d'ye think?" Little Jane poked him and smiled.

Then, as he began to speak, she edged in closer to listen.

Also by Adira Rotstein

Little Jane Silver
A Little Jane Silver Adventure
978-1554888788
$12.99

Little Jane Silver is the granddaughter of the notorious pirate Long John Silver. Growing up on her parents' ship, she vows to become a real pirate. As her ship is pursued by a mysterious pirate hunter, Little Jane tries to alert the crew to a devious saboteur on the ship, but by the time someone pays attention, it's too late.

More Great Fiction
for Young People

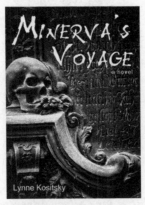

Minerva's Voyage
by Lynne Kositsky
978-1554884391
$12.99

Robin Starveling, aka Noah Vaile, is scooped off the streets of seventeenth-century England and dragged onboard a ship bound for Virginia by the murderous William Thatcher who needs a servant with no past and no future to aid him in a nefarious plot to steal gold.

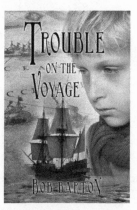

Trouble on the Voyage
by Bob Barton
978-1926607108
$10.95

In 1631, eleven-year-old ship's boy Jeremy finds himself
on the merchant ship *Henrietta Maria*, which has been
trapped in the ice of Hudson Strait for two months.
When the vessel finally breaks free, the crew members
resume their search for a northwest passage. But the ship
is leaking badly and the sailors are ravaged by scurvy. Will
anyone survive in this cold and desolate place?

Visit us at
Dundurn.com
Definingcanada.ca
@dundurnpress
Facebook.com/dundurnpress